No one wants to end up #RIP with 45 likes — your death turned to someone else's fleeting social capital, your last inane status update being the one that defines you for all time, your Friends' competitive grieving, and misery tourists perusing your profile... but that is probably what will happen, as Facebook has become the *channel for broadcasting news of the newly deceased, with the number of memorialized accounts soon to eclipse accounts of the living.*

Mark Zuckerberg is a merchant of death!

Whether it's the demise of another geriatric celebrity, or your best friend from college, taking a pill and jumping off a roof, nothing makes your News Feed blow up like someone's death. Then there's the rush to post long, dolorous status updates mourning their passing, tag the deceased in lo-res photos, and share their favorite songs as YouTube links.

Facebook claims the dead as its own, commodifying misery and fitting it seamlessly into its usual agenda: stalking your online shopping habits, advertising clothes, confusing politics, and wondering why you haven't had a baby yet.

Set in a London where Mick Jagger's kids rule the social scene, DEATH *and* facebook *is a true account of a doomed, dysfunctional love affair, posthumously pieced together from archived facebook posts, email, and SMS. A depressingly contemporary cautionary tale for our current depressingly contemporary times.*

DEATH

&

facebook

IPHGENIA BAAL

We Heard You Like Books • Los Angeles, California

PUBLISHED BY WE HEARD YOU LIKE BOOKS

A Division of U2603 LLC

5419 Hollywood Blvd, Ste C-231 Los Angeles CA 90027

http://weheardyoulikebooks.com/

Distributed by SCB Distributors

ISBN: 978-0-9964218-8-1

Copyright: © Iphgenia Baal 2018

A previous edition of this book was published in the UK by Bookworks under the title *Merced Es Benz*, 2016.

June 2018

First Edition

10 9 8 7 6 5 4 3 2 1

DEATH

&

facebook

Facebook User

Before we got together, Facebook User was a peripheral on my social scene. We knew some of the same people, and I'd run into him at parties, but we weren't what you would call friends — as in, I never had his number, and he never asked for mine. Then, early one November morning, he popped up on Facebook, commenting on a status update I'd posted, minutes before.

The public comment was quickly followed, by a monosyllabic private message. I replied, with just as terse a response. And so began a 'conversation' that continued, on and off over the next few days. The end result was us making a plan to meet, in 'real life'. I told Facebook User I was meeting friends for a drink, at Bradley's Spanish bar, in Soho. He said he'd see me there.

I arrived at the appointed time to find my friends, aware of the online flirtation, gossiping about what was going on between Facebook User and me. Someone told me he talked about me all the time. Someone else told me we were 'kindred spirits', that he was the 'real deal', and that it was 'about time' we hooked up.

Two hours later, Facebook User still hadn't shown.

Someone told me to call him.

I drunkenly obliged.

He answered after two rings.

'Hullo?' Facebook User said, 'who is this?'

It was strange, having spoken to him so much, only now hearing his voice.

Facebook User told me he'd been dragged to the other side of town and wasn't gonna make it. I could hear, from the background noise, that he was in a bar.

As soon as I got off the phone, everyone was full of questions. Too embarrassed to say I'd been stood up, I pretended to go to the toilet and left without saying goodbye.

I jumped on a bus, intending to go home, but when we reached Shoreditch, the driver announced the route was terminating.

I was waiting at the bus stop when Facebook User rang again. He said he was in the Russian club in Dalston, and that I should come there. As he said it, a bus which would take me to the bar arrived. It seemed like fate, so I got on, and told Facebook User that I'd see him there.

I arrived to find Facebook User in the company of a big, rowdy group of people, who'd been up since the night before, doing coke and balloons. They raised their eyebrows when he kissed me on the cheek, nudged one another when he got me a chair, teased him when he went to the bar to get me a drink. They catcalled, and hollered, when he kissed me.

In the beginning, things between us were good. It felt like it was meant to be; we'd played in the same playgrounds, peed in the same pools, might've waved from passing pushchairs, the result being a shared sense of reality, and humour, rooted in a sneering contempt for London life.

But if our backgrounds were similar, our present day situations were not. Facebook User had money and lived in a big house with Mick Jagger's kid, whereas I lived alone in a council flat, paying my rent with housing benefit.

I was used to being around people with money — a lot of my friends were trust fund kids, who I'd deride, forcing them to buy me drinks as reparation, because their money came from slave-trading shit, and I was black. My friends who didn't have money, and had to work, would receive condescending lectures explaining why they were wasting their time, and how the future promised a workless society, where the only endeavours of any worth were the things people did out of love.

But Facebook User was neither a rich kid, nor had he taken a position in the hierarchy of exploitation (aka, got a job). His was a criminal enterprise, which came complete with a spiel about Third World debt and a stressful gangster routine, where he bemoaned the guilt of selling death, and the weight of responsibility that came with understanding how this cold, hard world really worked. He played a baby Escobar, sloshing money around amongst his friends — he paid for a guy he knew from school to get a new kitchen fitted, and bailed out a girl he used to date, who was being chased by bailiffs. Something he *never* stopped bragging about.

I was impressed — I didn't know how to call up a soldier and order kilos of heroin to be delivered by chinook.

I started having fantasies about being a gangster's girl, flying around in helicopters, and being given wads of cash and expensive presents in return for keeping my mouth shut.

As you can imagine, things unravelled pretty fast.

I started voicing my concerns about what Facebook User did for a living.

We started having fights.

Facebook User stopped inviting me out with his friends.

He'd turn up at mine at 5am, wasted and unannounced, to fuck.

Torn between a genuine concern for his health and mental wellbeing, and feeling jealous at being left out, I started to stalk him on online.

I scoured Facebook for information about what he was doing and who he was with.

The more I stalked him, the less I liked him.

His drug-dealing mates were morons, and his posh friends were the sort of boarding school brats I'd always despised.

All romance went out the window, taking with it any hope I'd had that one day he'd come good.

He wasn't a badman.

He wasn't a G.

He was just another aspirational middle-class twat, who'd pretended to be something he wasn't, to get into my knickers.

Operating under the umbrella excuse of having been 'deceived', I fell into a classic victim routine. I bombarded Facebook User with emotional blackmail and empty threats about shopping him to the police. Facebook User ignored my messages, stopped answering calls, then deleted me on Facebook.

I made a PMS-crazed cyber-feminist strike, and posted his number to Craiglist, posing as a teenage girl looking for sex.

That got his attention.

Within minutes of the ad going live, I recieved a string of angry texts, and when I went on Facebook, I found that he'd blocked me.

I took down the ad, then tried to call to tell him I was sorry, but the number was dead.

I sent reams of email. Some pleading to let me make it up, others brimming with accusation, but when Facebook User ignored it all, I had to accept that I'd gone too far.

It was over.

The way I dealt with the fallout, publicly, was to shit talk Facebook User to anyone who would listen. I'd talk freely about his drug-dealing, hoping it'd get him in shit. I'd tell people how he couldn't get it up and would plead for me to suck his dick. I'd tell people how he hated being naked, because his legs were too short for his body, and how he'd put his jeans on when he got out of bed, even if it was just to go to the toilet.

I continued to frig myself off, recalling our first fumbled fucks, and I continued to Facebook stalk him, making friends with his friends, and checking their profiles for any sign that they were with him.

On Friday 13th July, about a month after we'd stopped speaking, I got a Facebook invitation from one of Facebook User's friends to a party happening that night in Hoxton Square. Knowing Facebook User would be there, I toyed with the idea of turning up.

I copied and pasted the event's address into Google. Google listed it as the old school building on Hoxton Square. GoogleMaps pinpointed its location. Websites of local papers ran the news it was being sold. An anti-gentrification blog protested the sale.

I closed the tab, returning to the event page, and started reading through the stupid Internet pseudonyms of people on the guestlist.

- Jimbo Mutant Shinobi
- Craig Knight Messman
- Ace Gunshot
- Laz Tafari
- G-Wiz Ayesha
- MC Hugger
- Noushy Sharma
- Joshy Boom
- Slobadan Eastdulovich
- Luis Attawalpa Attawalpa
- Awale Ali
- Violet von Westerholtz

I moved the cursor over vvw's name — Facebook User had spoken about her to me. He said that she was fit and I wouldn't like her. Her profile picture proved him right on one count.

I only lingered over this triumph momentarily, as the first post at the top of her page was a photo Facebook User was tagged in. Because I was blocked, his name was greyed out. In the photo, Facebook User had his hands round a blonde girl's neck, pretending to strangle her — something I knew he only did to girls he liked.

I clicked in the comments box and typed, 'he hates blonde girls anyway', posted it, then deleted it straightaway. Any notion I'd had of turning up at Hoxton Square and having a romantic reunion was delusional. At best he would ignore me, at worst it'd be a horrible fight.

I returned to the Facebook event and RSVPed, 'Not Going'.

I had other plans. It was the opening of my friend MW's exhibition in Peckham. To take my mind off Facebook User, I decided I would walk there.

I left the house and walked through the estates, past the teenagers ganging outside the chicken shop, and the burly badboys washing their cars in the yard, and the kids racing around the walkways between flats, shrieking over lines of flapping washing. I turned onto Whitechapel Market, bubbling with Bengalis. I crossed the river at Tower Bridge. As soon as I was in south London, I started getting wolf-whistles and comments. An old Jamaican called me 'princess'. I thought 'fuck Facebook User'.

I arrived in Peckham to people spilling out of the gallery onto the pavement. Smoking and drinking and shouting.

I looked for MW, and found him inside talking to LL and ET.

They each kissed me on the cheek in greeting, then LL asked, straight off the bat, whether I was going to 'this rave'.

'The "rave"?' I said, making the quotation marks in the air with my fingers, 'd'you mean Jimmy-fucking-stupid-Jagger's party?'

As intended, ET sniggered at this.

Jimmy Fucking Stupid Jagger was a phrase ET and I had coined, a few weeks earlier. We'd been drinking on the roof of The Red Lion pub, and a conversation that begun with me moaning about Facebook User became a wider pontification about the fates of famous people's kids. No doubt nannied and boarding-schooled, then everyone not only thinking they knew who you were, but also knowing you were loaded, so assuming you'd buy the drinks. Three pints in, it'd got quite philosophical.

Final verdict: if you are a famous person's kid, you can never really be cool.

MW pointed out that the "rave" wasn't a rave, because AD's brother owned the building, and had leant it to JJ for the party before it was bulldozed and redeveloped into luxury flats, so it wasn't a rave because it wasn't illegal.

'I thought Facebook User and you were...' LL interrupted.

He crossed two fingers.

I felt my face flush.

LL looked smug and said, 'should I not ask?'

Reminding myself of VVW, I stated my defense as succinctly as I could.

'There are some people in life', I told LL, 'who you just hate.'

MW started to laugh, doing an impression of Facebook User, saying 'nah, nah, nah', and cutting the air with one arm like a rapper.

Pleased someone else had taken on the mantle of slagging off Facebook User, I had a look at the show.

MW's photographs of blue tarpaulins had pride of place. KL's 'Absent Father's Choir presents...' poster was on the far wall, next to LM's oil paintings. AP's stonecarving of a giant Mitsubishi pill had its own in a cabinet. DA's painted canvas, up behind the bar, read, 'the battle is long, the beast is fierce and we all die in hospital surrounded by paperwork and doctors'. At the far end of the gallery, someone had plonked a battered motor, its bodywork eaten away by rust.

'It's about', MW said, 'the pointlessness of it all.'

I felt my phone vibrate in my pocket, and taking it out, was surprised to see LF's caller ID — we hadn't spoken in months, since she'd warned me off Facebook User. She'd said me being Facebook User's girlfriend 'only encouraged him', and that we shouldn't go out. I'd told her she was a jealous cunt and to go fuck herself. That'd been when things were good. Now Facebook User weren't speaking, it was different.

I let the call ring off. Unlocking my phone, I saw I had 17 missed calls. Eight from BB, three from BF, and five from FC — people who'd all be at Hoxton Square. I guessed Facebook User had started blabbing about the crazy shit I did.

I went to get a beer, and stand outside.

LL left for Hoxton, followed by a gaggle of girls in floral leggings.

As they made a procession in the direction of the bus stop.

MW made a wanker sign at his back.

A girl's voice started screeching.

I turned to see BMC attacking her boyfriend, JM, who was cowering in a plastic chair.

She clawed at his face with her nails, then thumped him over the head with her bag, before someone pulled her off.

I didn't notice MW until he was standing next to me.

He stood so close that when he told me to check my phone, I jumped.

I guessed whatever it was about Facebook User, because of the earlier calls, but from the look on MW's face thought it seemed more serious than anything to do with me.

First I thought, he'd been arrested. Second, it'd serve him right.

MW started stammering how 'sorry' he was, 'for taking the piss', 'because he was clearly really deep into it, and I respect that, you know.'

Facebook User was dead.

A hush fell over the crowd as the news was whispered from person, to person.

MW tried to give me a hug, but I pushed him away and ran.

I ran up the Walworth Road before turning into an estate I knew, where I went and hid behind the bins. I thought I would cry, and forced out a couple of encouraging sobs, but the tears didn't come.

I didn't feel upset, I felt guilty.

I'd harangued him so much in recent months, it felt like it was my fault, as if my outpouring of abuse had driven him to it... like I'd texted him to death.

When it got dark, I left my hiding place, and walked back to the gallery.

The crowd had thinned out considerably.

What few people remained were sitting outside, huddled in tight discussion. MW left the huddle, asked me if I was alright, then what I wanted to do.

I told him I wanted to go home, and that I'd just come to pick up my jacket.

He followed me inside, saying he thought going home wasn't the best idea, that I should be with people who 'knew what was going on'.

Meaning, Hoxton Square.

10 minutes later, I was in the back seat of MW's car, heading for Hoxton. He was pissed, so drove like a maniac. Cutting the lights at Camberwell Green and taking the turning wide, I was thrown from one side of the back seat to the other, and hit my head on the door. For a second, I thought we'd crashed. When I realised we hadn't, I half-wished we had — both dead in the same night, people would say.

MW asked if I was okay. I sat up, and, caught my guilty reflection in the rear view mirror. Facebook User was dead, and I was making it all about me.

When we got to Hoxton, MW pulled up outside the front door of the old school. I'd thought he was gonna come in with me. When he swivelled round in the driver's seat, patted my knee, and wished me 'good luck', I realised he wasn't.

I got out the car, but stayed loitering on the pavement for some time. Unsure what information people had been given, so unsure what sort of reception I'd get, I was nervous about going in.

I'd almost decided to bail, when I heard Congo Natty's *Code Red*, one of Facebook User's favourite tracks coming from inside. It was the song I'd played the night we'd got together. It felt like a sign, a nod of approval from Facebook User, telling me this was where I should be.

As soon as I walked through the door, I was accosted by WC, a dog-faced heiress, who grabbed me and shrieked, 'My best friend is dead!', before being swept away by a gaggle of blondes brandishing Marlboro Lights. It took me a minute to recognise one as GMJ, because I'd only ever seen her looking pretty and modelly, but now she was a fright. Pale face, hair flat against her head, big bags under her eyes from crying.

'My best friend is dead,' she said as she floated past. Exactly the same words as WC.

I'd been braced for an assault of recrimination for the way I'd treated him, but these girls didn't only seem unaware that Facebook User and I had broken up, they didn't even seem to know we'd been together.

I walked up the corridor, which led me into what must've once been the old school hall. A stage was set up at the far end, and someone had written *WE LOVE YOU FACEBOOK USER* in large blue and pink spraypaint letters on every wall.

I looked around the room for someone I knew.

I spotted LL standing by the opposite speaker. Our eyes met. He looked away.

The band came on. JJ took the mic.

'This set goes out to Facebook User', he said, '...who lived three times harder and three times faster than anybody else'.

The band launched into their first dodgy heavy metal number.

I started doing the maths in my head.

Facebook User was 29 years old, so that meant 58, 87...

I felt hands on my shoulders, and BH yelled in my ear, 'you should be up the front! She should be up the front!' He pushed me into the moshpit that had formed in front of the stage. I came straight out the other side and went to stand by the speaker, from where I watched the rest of the show, jealous at Facebook User's friends totally losing their shit, unable to join in without feeling like a hypocrite.

After the band came offstage, I ended up sitting backstage with Facebook User's friends, where his final movements were pieced together.

There'd been the Jagger wedding on Wednesday, where he'd stayed up all night. He'd got a cab back to London the following day, then met people in Visions on Thursday night, bragging about having not slept. He went back to Chiswick, alone, in the early hours of Friday. He was found dead Friday afternoon, eyes open, music playing, bottle of vodka clasped to his chest. When paramedics arrived, they estimated time of death between 4-8am.

I left the conversation, went to the bathroom, and locked myself inside a stall.

A group of girls followed me in, and talked in front of the mirrors.

'It's a bit of a weird party', one of them said.

'Yeah, I think a good friend of the people who are putting it on died', said another.

'Do you know what happened?' the first voice said.

A third voice, which I recognised, said, 'Heroin overdose'.

No one had mentioned anything like this to me.

'Apparently', the third voice carried on, 'he was sniffing it to come down off the coke. It's like an inverse heart attack. Your heart rate drops too fast, which *tricks* your body into thinking it's dead... and that is what kills you'.

The girls clattered their way out of the bathroom.

I sat on the toilet in disbelief — there'd been multiple times when we were going out that I'd thought he'd been high. Times when he turned up at mine, as white as a sheet and couldn't get it up. I'd confronted him about it once, but because his denial had been so convincing — heroin was for 'losers', he'd 'never touch that shit', I'd never asked him again. I put his pallor down to the the strip lighting in the hall, and mistook his lack of stamina for affection.

Finding out that Facebook User was using heroin made me feel better.

It meant that Facebook User dying was Facebook User's own fault and nothing to do with me.

We were thrown out of Hoxton Square around 4am. Against my better judgement, I ended up at a house party back south. There were lots of people there I didn't know, and when I was introduced to them, I was described as Facebook User's 'widow'.

People sat around, sniffing bumps of K, clanking beer cans with Facebook User anecdotes: the time Facebook User bit SH's finger almost off in a jealous rage, after the band SH managed won a Brit, prompted lots of laughs, as did the story about him headbutting the bouncer outside The Box and ending up with blood running down his face. Most of it was new to me. Conversation turned to the fight at the Wheelbarrow, which had happened a couple of months before Facebook User and I got together. It'd been all anyone talked about for weeks. Some people told it as a drunken mistake, where the pint glass shattered in Facebook User's hand, but others said he'd smashed it on the bar intentionally, before plunging it into the guy's neck.

Listening to the details argued over again made me recall what I'd thought about it all the first time I'd heard it: that it was idle gossip, spread by the uninformed and should be disregarded.

I went into the next room, where people were dancing to music, coming out of the telly. I lay on the sofa, pulled my jacket over my face and tried to sleep.

Someone turned the music up.

A group of people on the other sofa started smoking crack.

People started arguing.

Someone tugged the sleeve of my jacket, and a nasal American voice said, 'you can't sleep here, it's a party'.

'Leave her alone', I heard AP say, 'f' fuck's sake, her boyfriend's fuckin' dead'.

I pulled my jacket off my face and sat up.

'He wasn't my boyfriend,' I said, but nobody heard, because at the same time, DH spat in AP's face, and the whole room exploded. AP floored DH with a punch to the side of the head. Everyone was shouting. DH shrieked, then sobbed, the caterwauled, and kicked AP in the shins. He grabbed her, dragged her up the hall, punching her repeatedly before throwing her out the front door. She banged on the door to be let back in, and was threatening to smash a window, when GT came down from upstairs, where I guess he'd been sleeping, and threw everyone out. I was glad of the chance to escape and left without saying bye to anyone.

When I got back to mine, I went straight to bed, but found I couldn't sleep.

Facebook User dead from a drugs overdose and all anyone could think to do was drugs.

I opened my computer.

Facebook was already open in the browser.

The News Feed refreshed...

The first post read was a hashtag RIP, the next a misspelled status update calling him a 'sweet angle'.

There were sad face emoticons, and broken heart emoticons, and hundreds of pictures: Facebook User as a scrawny kid, Facebook User as spotty teenager, Facebook User and a group of his friends in Visions on the night he died.

I clicked the image to make it bigger and scrutinised his jpegged face. As grey as his greyed-out name. Even blurry, you could see he looked ill.

I was about to close the computer in protest, when a notification went 'ding'.

LAA had tagged me in a picture, and it was a picture of Facebook User and me.

Facebook User wearing a bright green anorak, lunging towards the camera, beer can held up in the air. Me in my baseball jacket, on a stool beside him, grinning from ear to ear.

I sat staring at the picture, watching it harvesting 'likes'.

EC liked it, GH liked it, BH liked it.

BH sent me a message.

'hey gurl, glad you made it the other night. i didn't get a chance, but wanted to say that, as far as Facebook User was concerned, i think you might've been the one'. Followed by the addendum, 'whatever that's worth. Xx'.

Leaving the computer, warm, and whirring, on my chest, with the picture LAA had posted, and the message from BH on the screen, I put my fingers in my knickers. I thought about Facebook User kissing me at the Wild Life party in front of all of his friends. I thought about Facebook User lying on top of me in bed and groaning. I thought about Facebook User being dead, watching me frig myself off over him and came.

Then, in a foolish, death-obsessed, post-orgasmic haze, I searched for our private messages. It was still there, but instead of his name, it said 'Facebook User', and instead of his profile picture, there was only Facebook's generic grey silhouette.

DEATH

&

facebook

Facebook
Friday, 11 November 2011

Iphgenia Baal · Yesterday, at 11.03 pm
whenever i write things on facefuck, i can always imagine them being read out at a later date in court.
12 PEOPLE like this
~~Lux Tufari~~ · 8.40 am
paranoiiaaa
Facebook User · 8.40 am
all these little things trust me

Iphgenia Baal · 4.28 pm
i want a rudeboy. 1 whos proper and won't talk to me when i'm on my period.
4 PEOPLE like this
~~Carlota Olmo Grijalbo~~ · 5.15 pm
it's LIES they say they won't talk to you but secretly they wanna hold you and care for you YUK it's BEYOND rude
~~Patrick Kennedy~~ · 10.03 am
there were loads at harrow
~~Frida Roois~~ · 10.03 am
i know there was at least 1!
~~Ki Par~~ · 4.30 pm
get me one too hahaha
~~Facebook User~~ · 9.39am
haha is that wale?
~~Scotty Cunningham~~ · 9.44am
rudegyal?
Iphgenia Baal · 9.47am
wifey?

Facebook Messenger
Friday, 11 November 2011

8.54 am
Facebook User
oi

Iphgenia Baal
orite

Facebook User
sup?

8:55 am
Iphgenia Baal
getting rid of the last bit of a hangover
sending out apology texts for behaviour last night

Facebook User
oh gad welcome to my world
i'd be doing the same but lost my phone keys and jacket

Iphgenia Baal
a reprieve?

Facebook User
maybe
what u doing this weekend?

8:56 am
Iphgenia Baal
mi dun no.
u?

Facebook User
i'm tracking my shit down now but after that
???????

8.57 am
Iphgenia Baal
there's something in the back of my mind
but i can't recall
be somewhere sometime to meet someone

Facebook User
bet there is

Iphgenia Baal
more than you find in most

Facebook User
i hate that

8.58 am
Iphgenia Baal
wha?

Facebook User
that feeling of impending doom

Iphgenia Baal
hmm my brain feels like a warehouse

Facebook User
an empty one

Iphgenia Baal
hahaha a hipster's penthouse
one chair

Facebook User
haha

8.59 am
Iphgenia Baal
what bit of london do you reside in?
i always assume you live in chiswick

9.00 am
Facebook User
kentish town

Iphgenia Baal
with who?

Facebook User
jimmy and hype
used to be emma and luis too but thrush metal wasn't paying the bills
you?

Iphgenia Baal
me?
solo

Facebook User
go on luv

Iphgenia Baal
thank you

9.01 am
Facebook User
i feel like a slave here always cleaning up others shit
i always assume u live in camberwell
or some other shit hole

9.04 am
Iphgenia Baal
fuc u!
bow e3 blud

9.07 am
Facebook User
how the fuck can i not know where i was from 12 til 4am

Iphgenia Baal
where were you at 4am?

Facebook User
my friend reckons i wasnt where i thought i was

Iphgenia Baal
you should CCTV yourself

Facebook User
i need a tracker but i would probably lose that

Iphgenia Baal
microchip?
or you know you can request CCTV footage of urself from the council
they send it on VHS

Facebook User
wankers
just to make it hard

9.09 am
Iphgenia Baal
hahaha
well
i think it is more that bureaucracy makes everything slow to change

9.44 am
Facebook User
just found my jacket and keys no phone
so where do u live?

Iphgenia Baal
bow

9.48 am
Facebook User
u evaded that question

Iphgenia Baal
bow was my answer

9.49 am
Facebook User
someone told me u were abusing them recently
can't remember who
u were calling them african

Iphgenia Baal
hmmm dunoo
african?

Facebook User
and i think they were posh
and blonde

Iphgenia Baal
my general style of assault is confusion

Facebook User
it made me laugh
i think it was at the box

9.50 am
Iphgenia Baal
can't be
they've never let me in
thank god

Facebook User
hahahaaaaa
i took a leak on the front door on their opening night
and i threw up at the bar
good night actually
i did have a really fun time there on saturday
i reckon u would have too

9.52 am
Iphgenia Baal
maybe

Facebook User
u would have if u were with me grumpy cow
so when u gonna let me take u out then?

9.54 am
Iphgenia Baal
cute
tonight?

Facebook User
haha well.........

Iphgenia Baal
well well well

Facebook User
hahaaaaa ur not a patient one r u?

Iphgenia Baal

time takes care of itself and so do i

Facebook User

thats what happens to me if i haven't left london for a while
my patience deteriorates

9.56 am
Iphgenia Baal

maybe from now on we should just get in scraps with each other

9.57 am
Facebook User

i agree

9.58 am
i just got "u were a dick last night"

Iphgenia Baal

HA
found your phone then?

10.03 am
Facebook User

so fucking should have slapped me then
nope on someone elses

Iphgenia Baal

nice to know they care

10.07 am
Facebook User

that letter tho
superlative!!!

DEAR JEFFERSON,

I WANTED TO LET YOU KNOW ABOUT AN AWFUL SITUATION THAT HAP-
PENED TODAY AT COACHELLA I AM HERE WITH THE LOVELY AND TAL-
ENTED MATTHEW IRWIN. I AM SHOOTING A STORY WITH THE EQUALLY
LOVELY FRANCESCA BURNS FOR I-D WITH ANDREA DOING THE MAKE-UP
AND LYNDELL DOING THE HAIR.

YESTERDAY WE MEET UP WITH IPHGENIA WHO HUNG OUT WITH US AT
THE FESTIVAL AND WHO I THEN LET STAY OVER AT MY HOUSE AS SHE
WAS A FRIEND OF MATT'S FROM DAZED AND FOUND HERSLEF WITH NO
PLACE TO STAY.

THE NEXT MORNING WHEN I BROUGHT HER WITH US TO THE FESTIVAL
SHE COULD NOT GET IN WITH US THROUGH THE ARTIST BACK DOOR
AS SHE SOLD HER PRESS PASSES THE DAY BEFORE, WHICH IS NOT A WISE
THING TO DO IN REGARDS TO THE MAGAZINE. ONCE WE WERE IN MATT
CALLED HER ON FRAN'S PHONE WHICH SHE HAD LENT HER AD IPHGE-
NIA HUNG UP ON HIM AFTER CALLING HIM AN ASSHOLE FOR LEAVING
HER AT THE GATE. THIS COULD ALL BE CHOCKED UP TO STUPIDITY AND
IMMATURIITY EXCPET FOR HER ACTIONS LATTER ON WHERE SHE CAME
UP TO WHERE WE HAD ALL THE CLOTHES FOR THE SHOOT, MY COM-
PUTER AND CAMERA EQUIPMENT AND SHE CAUSED A SCEEN SCREAMING
AT MATT CURSING HIM OUT AND THEN THROUGH HER DRINK ALL OVER
HIM, THE CLOTHES AND MY COMPUTER. NEEDLESS TO SAY THERE IS NO
JUSTIFICATION FOR HER BEHAVIOR AT ALL. SHE JEAPORDIZED OUR
WHOLE SHOOT, OUR CREDITALS FOR THE FESTIVAL, AND SHE PREYED
UPON MATTHEW LIKE A RAVEOUS BOR WOULD A PIECE OF ROAD KILL.
FURTHER MORE I THINK EVERYONE SHOULD KNOW THAT SHE IS GOING
AROUND BRAGGING TO EVERYONE THAT SHE HAS PHOTOS OF 16 CELEB-
RITIES DOING COCAINE - SHE SAID THAT SHE TOOK PARIS'S PHOTO YES-
TERDAY AND HAS LILLY ALLEN AS WELL - MEANWHILE SHE IS RUNNING
AROUND WITH LILLY HERE LIKE BEST FUCKING FRIENDS - WHICH IS
GROSS AND PATHETIC - AND I THINK WE ALL KNOW WHAT KIND OF SHIT
COULD GO DOWN ON LILLY IS THIS PHOTO WAS LEAKED TO THE PRESS
EVEN ACCIDENTALLY BY HER. I WRITING THIS NOT ONLY BECAUSE I AM
ANGRY AT HER BUT BECAUSE I LOVE YOU JEFFERSON AND DAZED HAS
BEEN MY FAMILY SINCE DAY ONE - I FEEL LIKE SHE IS PLAYING WITH FIRE
AND JEOPARDIZING THE MAGAZINE'S NAME, I THINK YOU SHOULD FIRE
HER ASS AND NOT LOOK BACK.

LOVE, JEREMY

Iphgenia Baal
hahahaha you should see the guy that wrote it!!

10.08 am
Facebook User
thats why i love u
kind of like why people fancy penelope cruz in blow
prolix
my letter woul have
sorry
my letter would have read t
that fucking iphgenia her days r numbered
but u cant be that bad people need to man up i reckon

Iphgenia Baal
or step down

Facebook User
haha backdafuckup
always looking for a scrap aren't u?

10.09 am
Iphgenia Baal
u would've liked the statement my ex made to the police

Facebook User
meanie

10.10 am
Iphgenia Baal
right?

Facebook User
which ex had to call the cops on you?

Iphgenia Baal

didn't phone went in to the cop shop with print outs of emails

Facebook User

hahahaha turned up!!

see everytime i say how much i love u people come up with this mad stuff but mmmmmmm im not convinced

10.11 am

Iphgenia Baal

hahaha u should b

he was trying to say i was stalking him see

Facebook User

discredited himself

Iphgenia Baal

and put different dates on "incidents" like from when i trashed his prius said it was like 2 weeks ago but it was more like 2 months

Facebook User

r u trying to put me off u?

10.12 am

Iphgenia Baal

dur

Facebook User

besides a prius has so many enemies

it wouldn't stick

10.13 am

Iphgenia Baal

people in prius's always look like policemen

Facebook User
everyone has a motive
boy dem hahahaha
so what borro do u reside in?

10.15 am
Iphgenia Baal
bow
i keep sayin

Facebook User
hahahahaa
that went straight over my head
thought u were just making silly noises

10.16 am
Iphgenia Baal
i can usually just about control that

Facebook User
so how is bow?
i was in whitechapel yesterday is that close?

10.17 am
Iphgenia Baal
bow is best
and yes

Facebook User
good munch

Iphgenia Baal
i'm by viccy park on the 15th floor
can see all the way to wembley

10.18 am
Facebook User
u near east london mosque?
i was there

Iphgenia Baal
bit north like 15 minute walk
what were you doing there?

Facebook User
ahhh ok i like it round there
none of ur biz

Iphgenia Baal
do you have a job?

10.19 am
Facebook User
yep but its not a 9 to 5

Iphgenia Baal
wot is it?

10.21 am
Facebook User
i work for a trading company in dubai

10.22 am
Iphgenia Baal
weird

Facebook User
accounts
contracts
logistics

10.23 am
Iphgenia Baal
SO weird

10.24 am
Facebook User
yeah weird
i have to go to ladbroke grove and get my jacket and keys

10.25 am
Iphgenia Baal
there's a party west

Facebook User
yessy

Iphgenia Baal
that's what was in the back of my mind

Facebook User
long

10.26 am
Iphgenia Baal
pub on the harrow road

Facebook User
go on

Iphgenia Baal
mixed race mafia
but there might be haters

Facebook User
r u not gonna let me feed u?

10.27 am
Iphgenia Baal
o dear

Facebook User
Fuck u

Iphgenia Baal
we should go have a fight then leave...

10.28 am
Facebook User
u little bag of trouble i think if i rolled with u

Iphgenia Baal
we would get arrested?

Facebook User
one of us would make it
one wouldnt

10.29 am
Iphgenia Baal
HA YES

Facebook User
to the death?

Iphgenia Baal
the only way

Facebook User
i think im gonna have 5 wings and a mirinda for brekkie xxx

Google
Friday, 11 November 2011

british trading company dubai
About 52,700 results (0.66 seconds)

Trading company - cityindex.co.uk
Ad cityindex.co.uk/Open-an-Account_Now
4.5 * rating for cityindex.co.uk
Start Trading now with City Index! (Losses can exceed your deposits.)
Range of Markets Spread Betting Trade Commodities Forex Trading

International Blacklist of Bad Suppliers › SUPPLIER BLACKLIST
www.supplierblacklist.com/dubai.html
 Are you performing due diligence on Kehai Weiye Electronics Ltd from
Shenzhen China who sells IC? If you are planning to buy products from
them, be careful of Scams. You may want to read the below review of ...
About Us · Blacklisted Suppliers · Forum rules · Loss Recovery and Help

Top commodity trading firms: Smart money or bad business?
www.futurescag.net/10-global-commodity-trading-firms.html
10 top global commodity trading firms: Smart money or bad boys? The
smart money typically are the men behind the curtain ... trading firms
makes them substantially more robust to a financial crisis than important
financial institutions," like Wall Street banks or insurance companies, ...

Dubai's dark side targeted by international finance police | Business
https://www.theguardian.com › Business › Dubai
[Jan 23, 2010] [video]

Searches related to british trading company dubai
　list british companies uae　british companies in abu dhabi
　british companies in uae　uk construction companies in dubai

Facebook Messenger
Friday, 11 November 2011

3.06 pm
Facebook User
r u there?
i was sleeping

Iphgenia Baal
yes
was sleeping too

Facebook User
made me feel worse
i have to go to ladbroke grove to get my wallet and keys

3.07 pm
Iphgenia Baal
so u can lose em again?

Facebook User
i lost my wallet last week cancelled all my cards
the whole time it was in front of me on the table

Iphgenia Baal
saddo

Facebook User
deeeeeeeek head

Iphgenia Baal
i used to do that in my less classy days so i didn't have to pay
that or snap my card in 2

3.08 pm
Facebook User
so tonights on me then?
hahaha

Iphgenia Baal
don't worry
u'll get ur money's worth ;)

3.09 pm
Facebook User
that...is exactly what i am worried about
99% sure i know where my phone is

3.13 pm
Iphgenia Baal
did u dream it?

Facebook User
thats quite a result seeing as i lost my phone keys and jacket and got it
all back
no sadly didn't dream it
had a really disturbing dream actually
i attacked some girl i know
then attempted to kill someone in front of my mum
he did say he was going to burn her

3.17 pm
i still don't know where i was from 12-4 last night
someone just told me

3.19 pm
Iphgenia Baal
i dreamt i was a hooker and had to have sex with this massive black guy
who turned out to be a woman

Facebook User
hahahaha

Iphgenia Baal
who then tossed herself off and then told me she always wears a wig???
where were you last night then?

3.20 pm
Facebook User
some posh blonde cow's house
hahahahha

Iphgenia Baal
awful

Facebook User
im waiting to get my phone back to hear how i've behaved

3.22 pm
Iphgenia Baal
exciting

Facebook User
i know i am quite looking forward to this
how old are u?

Iphgenia Baal
29
why?

Facebook User
just wondering at what age i'm going to stop being ammoral

Iphgenia Baal
i reckon you are a moralist disguised as an amoralist anyway

Facebook User

waaaaaaa

Iphgenia Baal

how old are you?

Facebook User

28

Iphgenia Baal

well you survived suicide age

you'll probably be fine

3.25 pm

what posh blondes are you sniffin around these days?

Facebook User

i hate blonde girls

seriously not down with that

3.26 pm

Iphgenia Baal

i hate blonde boys so white

Facebook User

innit

i am seriously white right now it's sad

i havent been on holiday for ages

Iphgenia Baal

another cheap holiday in other people's misery

Facebook User

right

i was just about to ask u where u live again

Iphgenia Baal
that's bad

3.27 pm
Facebook User
today i spent a minute genuinely considering if i have slight brain damage
due to this 4 hrs i cant remember
i did drink all day and not eat

3.28 pm
Iphgenia Baal
why?

Facebook User
funeral drinking
i'm gonna go pick up my phone
so am i seeing u later?

3.33 pm
Iphgenia Baal
affirmative

3.34 pm
Facebook User
oh yeah send me ur number
i will write it on my hand
i won't call it hahaha

3.37 pm
Iphgenia Baal
easy to remember
good to drink-dial x

Facebook Messenger
Saturday, 12 November 2011

9.59 am
Iphgenia Baal
never had you down as such a gent xx

11.00 am
Facebook User
that's never happened to me before

Iphgenia Baal
wha?

11.01 am
Facebook User
cut lines out and they're all still there in the morning

Iphgenia Baal
only boring girls need cocaine
My
A
D
D
is natural

11.02 am
Facebook User
hahahahahahahaha
still makes a change

Facebook

Sunday, 13 November 2011

Iphgenia Baal · 4.55 pm

tupac was a tosser

3 PEOPLE like this

Facebook User · 5.17 pm

no he was not

~~Carlo Otere Grijalbo~~ > Iphgenia Baal · 10.22 am

it's u haha

The Ruts / Staring at the Rudeboys
Uploaded 05/09/09 by westlifehateclub
Released March 1980, backed with Love In Vain
Doubled as crossword puzzle [Comments 213]
This song is f**king... youtube.com

3 PEOPLE like this

Facebook User commented on ~~The Aviary Bar~~'s post

~~The Aviary Bar~~ · Yesterday at 9.40 pm

remember 'i' before 'e' except in budweiser

17 PEOPLE like this

Facebook User · 10.09 am

hahahhahahahahahahahaah

Iphgenia Baal · 9.30 am

the best business is nobody's business

2 PEOPLE like this

Facebook User · 3.23 pm

i have no idea what that means but it sounds intelligent

~~Boo Saville~~ · 3.40 pm

there's no business like nobody's business!

Facebook Messenger
Monday, 14 November 2011

4.26 pm
Facebook User
u want to come to this place with me when i go?

Iphgenia Baal
which place?

Facebook User
kettles yard
its a house full of art like

Iphgenia Baal
art like?
i like art like

Facebook User
art I like
but its an in the week daytime thing

Iphgenia Baal
lets do it

Facebook User
yeahhh
cambridge

4.27 pm
Iphgenia Baal
i am guessing you aren't allowed in charge of a motorvehicle??

4.29 pm
Facebook User
fool
got my own car

Iphgenia Baal
YOU FOOL
terrifying

Facebook User
hahahaha i've never had a point and only written off one car

Iphgenia Baal
how

4.30 pm
Facebook User
and that was before i had a license
my friend was pissed so i was driving him home at 2am and he was making so much noise i said ur gonna make me crash so he did that thing with the wheel but too much cos he was so pissed
too funny
not a scratch no seatbelts going about 70

4.31 pm
Iphgenia Baal
went into a...

Facebook User
a brand new golf gti with about 2000 miles on the clock
central reservation then the other side bish bash
4.32 pm

Iphgenia Baal
fun

4.34 pm
Facebook User
very fun but anyway i'm a good safe driver

4.35 pm
Iphgenia Baal
i wasn't worried
i've never driven a car. a plane and a ferry but no car

4.36 pm
Facebook User
a plane?
i really want to do lessons but i love helicopters and i've never been in one

Iphgenia Baal
i went over ground zero in one when it was all still burnt out
pissed everyone else off by yelling 'we're all gonna die' lots of times

4.37 pm
Facebook User
how did u manage that?

Iphgenia Baal
it was some gay tourist thing
the guy i was with thought it would be romantic

Facebook User
hahahaaaaaaaa i like his style
i'm gonna take her to see where thousands of people died screaming
i would have just taken u to a graveyard

4.39 pm
Iphgenia Baal
:)

Facebook User

were u not even genuinely scared??

4.40 pm
Iphgenia Baal

not at all

4.42 pm
Facebook User

i respect that not giving a fuck is rare

Iphgenia Baal

chaos never died. there is no good or evil etc etc

Facebook User

i want to call my daughter chaos
dont steal that

Iphgenia Baal

eternal primordial? she'll probably be v well-behaved

4.45 pm
Facebook User

will she fuck

Iphgenia Baal

will she fuck? probably
hopefully

4.46 pm
Facebook User

hahahhaha i want to call my son gold and silver 100%

Iphgenia Baal

2 sons? or 1 name?

4.48 pm
Facebook User
1 name

Iphgenia Baal
doesn't stand a chance in the playground

4.49 pm
Facebook User
well i was thinking twins gold and silver but the likeliness of twins

Iphgenia Baal
do they run in the family? i've got em in mine

4.50 pm
Facebook User
fuck u've got twins in ur family!! turning into a real prospect!!

4.51 pm
Iphgenia Baal
but gold is better than silver it seems unfair + u've loved me since forever
Eu was telling me the other day 'he talks about you like you're a princess'

Facebook User
but i would rather be called silver the oldest can have gold
cos you're just so sweeting + enchanting!

4.52 pm
Iphgenia Baal
yes that works maybe the next set can be black and blue
stalker!

Facebook User
yeah i'm obsessed with u!!!! but no chaos and locust
i'll send them africa for the first five years for training

4.56 pm
Iphgenia Baal
family of freaks

Facebook User
my sons r gonna bang ur daughters

Iphgenia Baal
FUCK off

Facebook User
they will tho

4.57 pm
Iphgenia Baal
fuck you

Facebook User
why? scared of the freaks?

Iphgenia Baal
i don't like the idea of my unborn daughters being pimped out

Facebook User
coming for ur daughters hahaha or maybe i will name them after you

5.00 pm
Iphgenia Baal
I've never liked the whole kids named after their parents thing.

Facebook User
don't get too comfortable there
u ain't got me yet

Facebook
Tuesday, 15 November 2011

Facebook User > Iphgenia Baal

is this ur estate?? https://www.youtube.com/watch?v=qVaPUACUQnc

 **ROMAN ROAD E3 BLACK & RED HOOD**
Video by @49th media Uploaded 23 Sept 2010 by николай морозов (London) 171 views 14 comments happy birthday bruv [1] moist guys [2] UK gangsters = fagets youtube.com

Iphgenia Baal · 12.57 pm

first thing's first fuck everyone = amazing start

Facebook User · 12.59 pm

u should go out with him

Facebook User · 12.59 pm

ur style

Iphgenia Baal · 1.04 pm

hmmmmm i dunno

Iphgenia Baal · 1.05 pm

i think he's probs the one who threw dogshit at the granny

Facebook User · 1.06 pm

like i said

Facebook User · 1.06 pm

ur style

Iphgenia Baal · 1.12 pm

funnily enough i am at this exact moment helping my publisher write a letter of apology to groucho after he shat himself in the lobby

Facebook User · 1.12 pm

haHAAAA

Facebook User · 1.12 pm

gigi?

Facebook Messenger
Tuesday, 15 November 2011

1.13 pm
Iphgenia Baal
not actually funny they beat him up

Facebook User
u know how i feel about bouncers

1.15 pm
so am i gonna see you tonight?

Iphgenia Baal
dunno i think my friend from bristol is coming to stay

Facebook User
errrrrrr i used to live in bristol

Iphgenia Baal
why?

Facebook User
uni apparently

Iphgenia Baal
bet that worked out a treat

Facebook User
it was a 1 essay in 1 year affair

Iphgenia Baal
that was pretty much my gcses and look at me now!

1.18 pm
Facebook User
big in the game

1.19 pm
Iphgenia Baal
i write other peoples essays for ££££

Facebook User
isn't that illegal?

Iphgenia Baal
maybe not illegal but def cheat

Facebook User
the educational black market
i like it

1.20 pm
Iphgenia Baal
yes haha i'm an academic don

Facebook User
ha try this... topdocumentaryfilms.com/thieves-by-law

Thieves By Law Doc about the uppermost echelons of Russian criminal society; TBL have no right to family, registered address, or belongings. Several noted figures currently wanted by Interpol are interviewed.
Rating: 7.36 / 10 from 11 users youtube.com

i've gotta go but maybe c u later??

Iphgenia Baal
yes you will x

Facebook Messenger
Wednesday, 16 November 2011

10.51 am
Iphgenia Baal
what happened to you?

Facebook User
sorry babe meant to call didn't make it

10.53 am
Iphgenia Baal
i gathered as much

Facebook User
managed to spend 190££
what an idiot

Iphgenia Baal
loser!

10.55 am
Facebook User
big time

Iphgenia Baal
on what?

Facebook User
2g 120 booze taxi home

Iphgenia Baal
i spent £3.60

Facebook User
hahahah on?

10.56 am
Iphgenia Baal
half a pint and a bus fare home

10.57 am
Facebook User
owwwwww i need to hang around with u more

3.36 pm
Facebook User
meeting some people in town inna bit cinema
wanna come?

Iphgenia Baal
hmm really depends who. i am so jaded...

3.39 pm
Facebook User
why?

Iphgenia Baal
why so jaded?

3.40 pm
Facebook User
yes

Iphgenia Baal
?

Facebook User
why so jaded

3.41 pm
Iphgenia Baal
general fear of crowd dynamics/gang mentality
+ u hang out with loads of tossers

3.44 pm
Facebook User
hahahahaha u know too much

3.47 pm
but there're a lot of underachievers in my gang u'll feel right at home

Iphgenia Baal
what is it
first they ignore you, then they ridicule you, then they attack you and
want to burn you and then they build monuments to you and that is
exactly what is going to happen.

Facebook User
hahahahahahaaaaaaa
so u gonna come or not ??

3.49 pm
Iphgenia Baal
not

4.00 pm

Facebook User
WTF is ur problem today?

4.15 pm
Iphgenia Baal
today i'm like iggy
no fun

4.22 pm
i reckon you should take me for a drink instead

4.34 pm
Facebook User
i think so too but this hangover doesn't

Iphgenia Baal
hangovers only last til it gets dark

4.44 pm
Facebook User
i think i was kicked
how else do u fuck up ur calf?

Iphgenia Baal
walking into low tables?

Facebook User
backwards?

Iphgenia Baal
falling down stairs?

Facebook User
but surely something else would be hurting

4.56 pm
Iphgenia Baal
everybody hurts
REM

Facebook User
rem?
i'm slow today

4.58 pm
Iphgenia Baal
R.E.M.

Facebook User
??

Iphgenia Baal
it's an indie joke

5.01 pm
Iphgenia Baal
nirvana, nevermind x

Google
Wednesday, 16 November 2011

military barracks southend drugs
About 150,000 results (0.07 seconds)

Brompton Barracks
1 review · Army Facility   Website
Dock Rd · 01634 829944   Directions

HMS President
1 review · Military base   Website
72 St Katharine's Way · 020 7480 7219   Directions
More military bases

Town drugs ring run by Somalis (From Echo)
www.echo-news.co.uk/.../4866818.Town_drugs_ring_run_by_Somalis/
24 Jan 2010 A SOMALI gang running a ruthless drugs ring in Southend
and Westcliff ... We have old military bases in the country that could &
should be ... 10 soldiers arrested after a raid by military police suspected ...

Heroin and crack recovered in drugs gang crackdown across...
www.essexchronicle.co.uk/Heroin-crack-drugs-Southend/story.html
22 Sep 2011 Police carried out raids on several properties in Southend
... found that men were picking on vulnerable women and using their
homes as a base to store and supply local users ...
Missing: ~~military~~

[PDF] Unwantedg U n S - Section 1 - Essex Police
https://www2.essex.police.uk/museum/thelaw/n_9606lw.pdf
Jun 22, 1996 BRITAIN'S Special of the Year for 1996 ... drugs searches
and a team of 18 Specials Butcher. Specials scheme has ... As well as our
military bases, there Quay to a personally carried device a officers and
families of Southend officers to the Public Order exercise at special ...

Facebook Messenger
Thursday, 17 November 2011

9.30 am
Facebook User
aaaaayyyyeeeeeeeeeeeeeeeeeeee

9.31 am
Iphgenia Baal
hello freak x

Facebook User
u want to come to a party on sat? but sat dec 3rd
i want to show u off

Iphgenia Baal
like a date?

Facebook User
e2 blud thats all i know
no wait thats a lie i do know more..........

9.38 am
Iphgenia Baal
you're very good at suspense

Facebook User
i was trying to invite u but u already have been

9.39 am
Iphgenia Baal
o
on facefuck?

Facebook User

yes u fucker

Iphgenia Baal

i think i declined i don't pay

Facebook User

cow i will get u in for free...

Iphgenia Baal

neat

Facebook User

neat !!! hahahahha

Iphgenia Baal

i will get myself kicked out for free

Facebook User

hahahahah i will get myself kicked out for free is MASSIVE
but i reckon its gonna be one of those anything goes spots

9.41 am

Iphgenia Baal

what? even picking mercilessly on blonde posh girls?

Facebook User

ur fav

Iphgenia Baal

my main source of entertainment :)

9.44 am

Facebook User

i dont think theres gonna be that much of that

Facebook
Thursday, 17 November 2011

WILD LIFE   436 invited
11.00 pm 3rd Dec - 5.00 am 4th Dec 2011   122 going
Cremer Street London E2, United Kingdom   13 maybe

WILD LIFE
Save the date in ur diary. Want 2 c big firm out - ull prob have to keep
the 4th clear 4 recovery...r u in??? - with **Facebook User**, ~~Jimbo Mutant~~
~~Shinobi~~ and 30 others
12 PEOPLE like this
WILD LIFE · 8.45 pm
can't tag all at once add some names to let the gang know!!!!
WILD LIFE · 8.49 pm
~~Sam Cowley, JTG Rovner, Dan Nordelli~~ u rolling??
~~Chris Jones~~ · 8.52 pm
Tribes Unite
~~Chris Jones~~ · 8.52 pm
ROOOOLLLLLLLLLLLLL OOOOUUUUTTTTTTT!!!!!!!!
WILD LIFE · 8.55 pm
representing with the names
~~Laura Tibbs~~ · 9.05 pm
oui oui oui
~~Alice Wawrin~~ · 9.12 pm
Back 2 beefa!!!
~~Aaron Freeman~~ · 9.13 pm
knob lol x
~~Jake Moran~~ · 9.45 pm
baaaaaaaare spicy
WILD LIFE · 9.45 pm
yeeeeeeeaaaaaaahhhhhhhh fuk da dowtas

Facebook Messenger
Friday, 18 November 2011

3.29 pm
Iphgenia Baal
i wish i could just run away today

Facebook User
where would you go?

Iphgenia Baal
addis ababa

3.30 pm
Facebook User
ahhhhhh i was in ethiopia last year
planning on going back soon

Iphgenia Baal
I&I

Facebook User
what is I&I?

3.31 pm
Iphgenia Baal
oneness with god

Facebook User
okay

Iphgenia Baal
u know as in I&I

jah rastafari
flying
lion
zion
never had u down as being so whitie

3.32 pm
Facebook User
ahhhhhhhh iyani
bless
the rasta across the road called me killa king lion fam the other day

3.33 pm
Iphgenia Baal
bless indeed
i saw a dread yesterday who had dyed his locks green

Facebook User
powerful look

3.34 pm
Iphgenia Baal
i think incognito suits you better

Facebook User
i'm so white right now it sad

Iphgenia Baal
repatriate from the inside?

3.35 pm
Facebook User
going to australia on xmas day actually
to see the fam

Iphgenia Baal
little abbo
for how long?

3.36 pm
Facebook User
5 weeks so fay
*far
but maybe 7

3.38 pm
Iphgenia Baal
u never said

Facebook User
didn't i?

Google
Saturday, 19 November 2011

flight australia xmas day
About 462,000 results (0.56 seconds)

Why miss out? Fly to Australia with deals you won't find online
Ad www.dialaflight.com/Australia
5.0 rating for dialaflight.com *****
Book flights to Australia today!

Flights To Australia £1559 | Flightcentre.co.uk
Ad www.flightcentre.co.uk/AustraliaFlights
4.5 rating for flightcentre.co.uk *****
Lowest Airfare Guaranteed For You Call Our Experts & Get Quotes!
Compare 80+ Airlines · Offers Updated Daily · ABTA Protected
       Flights to Sydney
       Flights to Brisbane
       Flights to Perth

Boxing Day Flight Sales: Fares from £55 | finder.com.au
https://www.finder.com.au › Boxing Day Sales
Jan 9, 2017 - Find the best Boxing Day flight sales in 2016. Save on
domestic and international flights from Virgin Australia, Emirates and
Jetstar. Buy BARGAIN LAST MINUTE cancellations from London
Gatwick, London Heathrow...

Customs: Export-Import Procedures by Customs of Australia
https://australia.visahq.com/customs/
Free import if you are aged 18 years or over • 250 cigarettes • 2.25 litres of
alcohol • up to A$900 worth of general goods (gifts, souvenirs, cameras,
electronics, leathers, perfume, jewellery, watches.) Prohibited • Firearms,
weapons and ammunition • Medicinal products • Protected wildlife

Facebook Messenger
Saturday, 19 November 2011

8.14 pm
Iphgenia Baal
i don't want you to go

Facebook User
i know!!
been looking forward to this trip for so long and now uuuu

8.18 pm
Iphgenia Baal
take me with u xxxxxx

Facebook

Sunday, 20 November 2011

Facebook User · 5.38 pm
LOST MY PHONE - IT'S STILL RINGING!!!!!!!!!!!
10 PEOPLE like this
~~Clara Saunders~~ · 5.38 pm
i told u to give up on yesterday
Facebook User · 5.41 pm
i know i know should've listened to the oracle
Facebook User · 5.41 pm
temporary 07747 665 434

Facebook User liked ~~Clara Saunders~~'s link
Citizens of Nowhere | The Evil of Statelessness
The evil of neoliberal globalization and the revolting corporate dream:
people's spatial positioning in relation to media and the Crisis of the state
in a Digital Age
3 PEOPLE like this
~~Clara Saunders~~ · 5.44 pm
so good seeing you last night xxx

~~Stu Dee~~ > **Iphgenia Baal** · 11.22 pm
do you know if this is real?
"Everything we call real is made of things that cannot be regarded as real."
NIELS BOHR 7 | 10 | 1885 – 18 | 11 | 1962
3 PEOPLE like this
~~Luis Atawalpa Atawalpa~~ · 11.57 pm
fuck yeah!!!
Iphgenia Baal · 11.59 pm
.... so, no
~~Luis Atawalpa Atawalpa~~ · 11.57 pm
????

Facebook Messenger
Monday, 21 November 2011

9.37 pm
Iphgenia Baal
got an earful from laura last night !!

Facebook User
yaaaaawn what did she have to say this time?

Iphgenia Baal
she told me u were nothing but trouble!!!

Facebook User
woman needs medicating

Iphgenia Baal
haha
i told her that it is funny

9.39 pm
Facebook User
what is?

9.42 pm
Iphgenia Baal
how the same we are
they r genuinely worried hahaha

Facebook User
the difference between you and me is that you spazz out every weekend
for no fucking reason while i hold my shit down for years at a time but
when i do lose it people get hurt

9.45 pm
Iphgenia Baal
body count?
zero

1022 pm
Iphgenia Baal
u r a sweeeeetie
i kno this!

Facebook Messenger
Thursday, 24 November 2011

11.04 pm
Facebook User
why's everyone saying florence is a racist?
someone told me she fucked drake the other day
thats prob why she is now

Iphgenia Baal
fuck a duck
who is drake?

11.06 pm
Facebook User
some gay rapper/singer
the one who sounds like a computer?
he's almost turned me into a racist

11.07 pm
Iphgenia Baal
just looked him up
poor flo
so embarrassing

Facebook User
asking for it if u ask me

11.08 pm
Iphgenia Baal
u think everyones asking for it

11.09 pm
Facebook User
i made a loaf of bread the other day

11.12 pm
Iphgenia Baal
THAT is more the kinda thing i'm into

Facebook User
wait for it......
garlic, onion, rosemary and chilli and polenta in the mix
lasted 10 mins in this house

Text
Friday, 25 November 2011

10.49 am
Facebook User
owwwwww u coming west today

Iphgenia Baal
i may well

10.53 am
Facebook User
go on
u know u want toooo

Facebook Messenger
Friday, 25 November 2011

12.03 pm
Facebook User
just went downstairs and there was thanksgiving munch in the fridge

Iphgenia Baal
nice

Facebook User
it spun me out i ate so fast
there was candied yams and pecan pie and pumpkin pie

Iphgenia Baal
i love leftovers for breakfast...
i was gonna make buttermilk pancakes

12.04 pm
Facebook User
i would swap that cold food is not the one
but that pecan pie was something else
but my fridge is too cold so takes the taste away

12.11 pm
Iphgenia Baal
turn it down?

Facebook User
i should really

Iphgenia Baal
or is it up?

Facebook User
but i like cold milk
really cold milk

12.12 pm
Iphgenia Baal
fussy.
put it at the back
or in the freezer?

Facebook User
frozen is too cold iffy

Iphgenia Baal
you can put it in just for a bit before you drink it
or take it out a bit before

12.13 pm
Facebook User
u know that's not practical
plus the number of cans of coke i have exploded in that fridge
and it looks like a dirty protest that is the worst thing

eMail
Saturday, 26 November 2011

9.02 pm
Iphgenia Baal
me rofling x
[Attachment: Photo674.jpg]

Facebook User
v. cute

10.00 pm
Iphgenia Baal
me doing something else ;) ;)
[Attachment: Photo675.jpg]

10.02 pm
Facebook User
yesssy

10.10 pm
Iphgenia Baal
so am i seeing u later??? xxx
[Attachment: cocoa tea — 18 and over.mp3]

10.23 pm
Facebook User
yes yes for sure x

Text
Monday, 28 November 2011

1.24 pm
Facebook User
hello baby

Iphgenia Baal
hihihihi

Facebook User temp
hello hello

1.25 pm
Iphgenia Baal
u r cute xxx

Text
Tuesday, 29 November 2011

8.20 pm
Facebook User
come meet me x

Iphgenia Baal
where ru?

Facebook User
ur fave place

Iphgenia Baal
?

8.21 pm
Facebook User
the box come
i will get u in this time x

9.23 pm
Iphgenia Baal
walking up from the bus stop
should i get into the queue?

9.47 pm
hello???
answer ur phone pls

9.55 pm
you kno what? forget it!
u r an idiot

.

10.19 pm
Facebook User
i'm sorry i'm sorry
please come back!!!
i'll wait for u outside x

10.22 pm
Iphgenia Baal
i'm on bus home

10.27 pm
Facebook User
get off then!

Iphgenia Baal
what the hell?

Facebook User
i'm going outside to wait for u NOW!!!
and i'm not going back in til you get here

10.33 pm
i'll freeze to death if you don't come back

10.35 pm
Iphgenia Baal
ok ok u bloody bastard x

10.42 pm
so answer ur phone!!!

11.52 pm
you are such a fucking selfish idiot UNBELIEVABLE
thanks for nothing!

Text
Wednesday, 30 November 2011

12.21 am
Facebook User
where are you then?

Iphgenia Baal
whhere were you?

Facebook User
pick up x

Iphgenia Baal
no

Facebook User
don't b a dickk

9.26 am
Iphgenia Baal
I WANT TO FUCKING KILL YOU XXXX

Facebook User
was i supposed to call u?

Iphgenia Baal
we were supposed to meet

Facebook User
yes yes sorry was punched
call u ina bit

Text
Thursday, 1 December 2011

11.11 am
Iphgenia Baal
i've been calling u all morning. y u no answer my calls?

5.19 pm
Iphgenia Baal
u slept all day?

Text
Friday, 2 December 2011

11.01 am
Facebook User
i tried to call but you didn't pick up

Iphgenia Baal
missed it

11.12 am
so answer then
u r anitemare

11.30 am
Facebook User
what's anitemare?

Iphgenia Baal
haha r u being serious?

3.50 pm
Facebook User
i'm getting a cab to urs

Iphgenia Baal
i won't hold my breath

Facebook User
YES YOU WILL

Facebook Messenger
Saturday, 3 December 2011

7.17 pm
Facebook User
meeting peeps at a pub off hoxton sq but don't worry i've prepped them
told them all not to be freaked out by my first serious girlfriend xx

7.23 pm
Iphgenia Baal
hahaha r u drunk?
also, who are them?

Facebook
Monday, 5 December 2011

WILD LIFE added 78 photos to the album **HXTN** — with **Iphgenia Baal** and **Facebook User** · 10.13 am

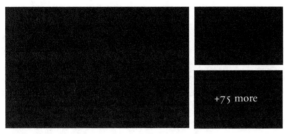

27 PEOPLE like this

~~Awale Ali~~ · 10.13 am

yes mate. that's what you want – a strong mother for ur children

~~Max Goldfinger~~ · 10.13 am

shiiiit y didn't i no about dis????

~~Anoushka Sharma~~ · 10.14 am

cuuuuuuute bruv

~~Paul Feigelfeld~~ · 4.44 pm

What the fucks going on in Tehran???

Iphgenia Baal · 4.44 pm

"The invaders threw stones at windows, and one was seen with an apparently looted portrait of Queen Elizabeth II."

~~Nina Franz~~ · 4.47 pm

bogus insurrection

Iphgenia Baal · 5.09 pm

monday morning cash converters: stuff is just money you can't spend

3 PEOPLE like this

Facebook User · 5.54 pm

REAL

Facebook Messenger
Monday, 5 December 2011

5.01 pm
Iphgenia Baal
ur friends r waaaankers xx

Facebook

Tuesday, 6 December 2011

Iphgenia Baal changed her profile picture · 4.40 pm

12 PEOPLE like this

~~Nil Tomakan~~ · 5.02 pm

in or out?

Iphgenia Baal · 5.04 pm

if u have to ask u don't know me well enough

Iphgenia Baal · 5.07 pm

always out

~~Nil Tomakan~~ · 5.09 pm

<3

Iphgenia Baal · 5.15 pm

i was wrong about 2pac he's not a tosser but the person running his fb account is

13 PEOPLE like this

Facebook User · 5.25 pm

hahahahaha

Facebook User · 5.25 pm

2PAC for president!!

~~Paul Fiegelfeld~~ · 9.09 pm

I didn't choose presedential life presedential life chose me!!!

Text
Saturday, 12 December 2011

8.22 pm
Facebook User
what you doin this eve?

Iphgenia Baal
seeing you?

8.25 pm
Facebook User
cool
be with you shortly x

10.04 pm
Iphgenia Baal
how short is shortly??

10.10 pm
Facebook User
leaving now!!

Iphgenia Baal
where are you?

10.14 pm
Facebook User
Chiswick but i'm leaving.

10.24 pm
Iphgenia Baal
blanking my calls?

Facebook User
cab is on it's way don't stressssss x

10.26 pm
Iphgenia Baal
ok it's cool, i'm cool
see u innabit x

11.43 pm
Iphgenia Baal
are you okay?
where arrrrre you?

Text
Friday, 13 December 2011

12.00 am
Iphgenia Baal
be a dick then
i made you food and myself all pretty
could've done something else with my evening so thanks for wasting my
time!

1.22 am
Iphgenia Baal
u have fucking wound me up on purpose

2.01 am
Facebook User
not my fault

Iphgenia Baal
so WHERE ARE YOU?

5.35 am
Iphgenia Baal
actually you take the fucking piss. u r a joke. u've really upset me and for
what?

7.41 am
Iphgenia Baal
i haven't slept all night

8.43 am
Iphgenia Baal
now i'm just worried.

Facebook User

mash up sorry babe c

Iphgenia Baal

fuck u

9.03 am

Facebook User

come here

Iphgenia Baal

no

Facebook User

why not?

Iphgenia Baal

don't wanna be that girl

10.47 am

Facebook User

You are that girl dummy but you did that all on your own

Facebook

Friday, 13 December 2011

Iphgenia Baal · 8.12 am

https://www.youtube.com/watch?v=iU5L-Wc8-JY

Disappointed Bride — The Hearts
A great track from the 1960s all-female doo-wop group 'The Hearts', with which Zelma "Zell" Sanders began her record-producing career. She was one of... (78RPM Transfer) [2.29] youtube.com

~~Nat Atta~~ LIKES this

~~Danny Brady~~ added a new photo to the album: <u>Mobile Uploads</u> — with **Facebook User**, ~~Ben Shoesmith~~ and 7 others · 9.12 am

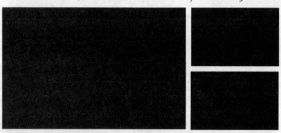

17 PEOPLE like this

~~Serena Mattar~~ · 9.12 am

sweeeeeeeeeeeeet

~~Ben Hypolite~~ · 9.13 am

D D D D DANGER

~~Danny Brady~~ · 9.17 am

corrosive

~~Ben Hypolite~~ · 9.20 am

northern grit

~~Ben Hypolite~~ · 9.23 am

pahahahahahahaha yes matey

Google
Friday, 13 December 2011

military smuggling drugs

About 647,000 results (0.49 seconds)

Military Smuggling Drugs - WantToKnow.info

www.wanttoknow.info/militarysmuggledheroin

Heroin smuggled in body bags of GIs reported by key military eye witness, 25-year DEA veteran, and a Wall Street... One of the couriers was a army major and the other an army master sergeant... Mike had to go underground for his own safety..

Soldiers jailed for selling smuggled Iraq weapons | UK news | The ...

https://www.theguardian.com › World › UK News › Military

Nov 24, 2007 - Two soldiers who smuggled stolen guns out of Iraq to sell as ... was "riddled with drug abuse and dealing" at the time of the incident three years ...

British soldiers 'smuggle heroin from Afghanistan' - The Week

www.theweek.co.uk/.../british-soldiers-'smuggle-heroin-afghanistan'

Detectives investigate UK troops thought to be smuggling drugs on military planes... returning from duty in Afghanistan involved in drug trafficking... army use of trafficked heroin - and the peddling of it - are found to be rife ...

MoD probes claim that soldiers are smuggling heroin from ...

www.dailymail.co.uk/.../Military-police-investigate-claims-British-troops

12 Sep 2010 - The claim that heroin and other drugs are being smuggled in by a handful... Military detectives launched the probe into "unsubstantiated" claims military aircraft... additional sniffer dogs as part of the crackdown at the bases.

Facebook Messenger
Saturday, 14 December 2011

5.16 pm
Facebook User
baal head

Iphgenia Baal
hi

5.17 pm
Facebook User
hiya

Iphgenia Baal
how was ur night?

5.19 pm
Facebook User
yes
very nice
drank tequila

Iphgenia Baal
with ur mum?

Facebook User
no u fuckin dickhead
when i got back to town

5.20 pm
Iphgenia Baal
i met a fan last nite

5.25 pm
Facebook User
ner

Iphgenia Baal
ner urself

Facebook User
so famous

5.28 pm
Iphgenia Baal
i i think i'll stick to notorious or perhaps just renowned

Facebook User
illustrious
i still have ur book. the paper oe
*one
i'm holding out that one day it will be worth loads

5.32 pm
Iphgenia Baal
u've got it but have u read it??

Facebook User
i've read the tramp story twice
brutal paranoid suffocating
very you
im on the one about someone called the pest now?

5.33 pm
Iphgenia Baal
um
is that good or bad?
i'm not sure

Facebook User
to a writer yes
to a girlf no
haha

Iphgenia Baal
ur mum?

5.35 pm
Facebook User
was good...
a nice little cottage in a nice little village
maybe i'll take u there one day
if ur good x

Text
Monday, 16 December 2011

6.09 pm
Iphgenia Baal
didn't mean to b rude but at the same time u make me come all the way
across town to see u + ur on ur way out...?
i don't understand why u think you can talk to me the way you do
it actually makes me feel sick

6.11 pm
and you neither want or try to respond!

6.36 pm
Facebook User
not my fault if the biggest rockstar in the world is para about his guestlist

6.55 pm
Iphgenia Baal
I don't give a shit about mick control freak jagger or his xmas stupid party

eMail
Tuesday, 17 December 2011

2.18 pm
Iphgenia Baal
mostly bored right now xxx
[Attachment: Photo25.jpg]

3.07 pm
Facebook User
do some work x

3.10 pm
Iphgenia Baal
i miiiiissssssss u alreadddddy xxx

Text
Wednesday, 18 December 2011

6.00 am
Facebook User
do u remember the first time we met?

7.02 am
Iphgenia Baal
don't remember meeting any of my boyfs for th2 first time ;)

Facebook User
rave on scrubs before carnival
2000?
2001?

7.04 am
Iphgenia Baal
hmmmm maybe

Facebook User
u were passed out
i helped u up

7.06 am
Iphgenia Baal
i think i remember

Facebook User
do you remember what i said?

Iphgenia Baal
???

7.10 am
Facebook User
you really don't remember?

Iphgenia Baal
i'm not sure
i remember the party
what did u say?

7.13 am
Facebook User
that u were the fittest girl i'd ever met
ha

7.16 am
Iphgenia Baal
i remember
just didn't remember it was you xxxx

Text

Friday, 20 December 2011

10.55 pm
Facebook User
I love fucking you too much

11.00 pm
Iphgenia Baal
ha. ur sweet!

Facebook User
no

Iphgenia Baal
no what?

11.03 pm
Facebook User
no I don't like it
ur in my head all day long

Text
Saturday, 21 December 2011

12.09 am
Iphgenia Baal
were u even listening to me last night?
u should b an artist
u've got a better idea of what's going on than most xxxx

12.11 am
Facebook User
i'm always listening and like i said
if I was born 50 years ago i would've but these days everyones at it so i am
doing something else
xxxxx

Facebook Messenger
Monday, 23 December 2011

4.19 pm
Iphgenia Baal
please come see me before u gox

Facebook User
i am trying

Iphgenia Baal
then try harder!

4.21 pm
Facebook User
listen everything in my life falls into 2 categories
things that I have to do that I don't want to and things that I want to do
that I can't

Iphgenia Baal
well how about you turn me into neither?

Facebook User
I am trying my best

Iphgenia Baal
sex+spaghetti?

4.27 pm
Facebook User
mmmhx

Facebook Messenger
Monday, 24 December 2011

10.20 am
Iphgenia Baal
today?? x

11.38 am
Facebook User
hopefully done by this eve x

Iphgenia Baal
well i said i'd be at my folks in the morning, so you could stay and go to the airport from here... maybe??

Facebook User
yeah sounds good. will call when done x

7.23 am
Iphgenia Baal
anywhere near done? x
also, what do u want for dinner?

7.37 am
Facebook User
thought we were all set for spaghetti? xx

Iphgenia Baal
haha ok x

Facebook

Monday, 24 December 2011

Facebook User was tagged in **Ben Fletcher**'s post · 10.42 pm
BIG UP W4 XMAS RAVING CREW !!!! MY BRAINS LIKE FUDGE
~~Awale Ali~~, ~~Anoushka Sharma~~, ~~Lemon Aid~~, ~~Ben Hypolite~~, ~~Lee Tafari~~,
~~Chelsea Leyland~~, Facebook User, ~~Craig Messiman~~, ~~Henry Diplo~~,
~~Harry Lloyd Jones~~, ~~Maria Duval~~, ~~Sean DipsetLuluPo~~, ~~Hassan Morhej~~,
~~Jimbo Mutant Shinobi~~, ~~G-White Ayesha~~, ~~Violet von Westerholtz~~

Iphgenia Baal · 10.57 pm
I wish there was a French foreign legion for girls
2 PEOPLE like this
~~Kevin What~~ · 11.01 pm
i feel like that today... booze is a fucker
Iphgenia Baal · 11.02 pm
no booze. endemic
~~Kevin What~~ · 11.09 pm
shit

~~Ace Gunshot~~ > Facebook User · 11.31 pm
only difference between government and gangsters = ur opinion
http://www.youtube.com/watch?v=DjOSof5TSn8&feature

Tupac Uncensored & Uncut Lost Prison Tapes
Never-before-seen interview at Clinton Correctional
Facility. Pac riffs on topics from his involvement in gang
life, to American prisons, and his relationship with his
mother. [Comments] TUPAC ALIVE 2019!!!!!!!

Facebook User · 11.44 pm
true dat
Facebook User · 11.45 pm
u shldnt b online bruv

Facebook Messenger
Monday, 24 December 2011

10.45 pm
Iphgenia Baal
u r totally selfish
goodbye
aka getfucked

Facebook Messenger
Sunday, 25 December 2011

2.32 am

Iphgenia Baal

anyway it is clear to me you are still bang at it

not that i believed you when you said you wanted to stop

just thought that maybe a little belief or encouragement wouldn't go amiss

this is just another nice little holiday from a lifestyle that you will keep at

til you die

emphasis on style

keeping up with the sort of people who will always always be around

you might read that as loyalty

but its not

2.39 am

its a choice Facebook User

about what sort of energies you want to have around you

it is not about the criminality of what you do

it's the double bluff junkie existence where everything becomes a lie

possibly the hardest thing to unlearn

and what eventually catches up with you

Facebook
Tuesday, 27 December 2011

Iphgenia Baal · 6.50 pm
spellcheck doling out life advice...

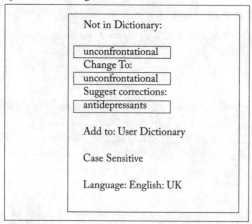

David Gates · 6.57 pm
you shouldn't stand for that. kick up a fuss
Iphgenia Baal · 7.00 pm
i changed the dictionary to English: Jamaican and now it says BUN DEM

Facebook User · 10.47 pm
Australian number 0435 179 276
7 people like this
Sofia Macciou · 11.36 pm
no one cares
Bellamy Burrows · 11.37 pm
hope you got in okay!!!! can't wait to have some fun!!!! xxxxxxx

Facebook Messenger
Wednesday, 28 December 2011

9.11 pm
Facebook User
hello? r u there?

Iphgenia Baal
why?

9.12 pm
Facebook User
i'm going to the toilet
tell me something for when i get back
anything

9.15 pm
Iphgenia Baal
people are saying that time will take care of people like me

9.24 pm
Facebook User
no i said that to u
i said people like u don't last long

Iphgenia Baal
i said that to you too!
besides, it was willie nelson...

Facebook User
cos u try so hard to piss everyone

Iphgenia Baal
no

9.26 pm
Facebook User
off it's like u want out

Iphgenia Baal
my methods leave something to be desired but my intent is impeccable

Facebook User
pfffffff listen i am sorry about not seeing you before i left but ur little
temper tantrum wasn't necessary however
we are cool
how can we not be?
but just realise that this is not about other people
you don't like living like this

9.34 pm
Iphgenia Baal
you lied about where you were + turned into an arrogant prick for no
reason

Facebook User
it happens
you have got to learn to deal with the fact that people are arseholes
why is that a surprise to you? doesn't mean they don't care
but im not gonna report back to you on my every move girlfriend or not
all that is important for u to know is that u should never EVER try and
flip on me today i decided that im not having a bar of that shit from
anyone from now on

Iphgenia Baal
so strict! i like it.

Facebook User

mate

im waiting for my friend to wake up and when he does im gonna tell him
if he ever

draws on me again im gonna stab him

9.47 pm
Iphgenia Baal
what did he draw?

Facebook User
swastikas and dicks

Iphgenia Baal
magic marker?

Facebook User
make up but it's not the point
i'm not a mug and it's probably the only time he can take me for one

Iphgenia Baal
u v. sweet when u sleep
finally silent

Facebook User
hahahaha fuck u

Text
Thursday, 29 December 2011

4.44 am
Iphgenia Baal
Do you miss me yet?

Facebook User
I miss ur bum

4.46 am
Iphgenia Baal
My bum misses you toox

eMail

Sunday, 1 January 2012

2.30 am

Facebook User

well? u fuckin liability?

5.12 am

Iphgenia Baal

oi boy. i lost my phone xxxx

6.10 am

Facebook User

and i sent u such a nice message. pisshead xxxx

[Attachment: Mavado - "Real Killer (No Chorus).mp3]

eMail
Wednesday, 4 January 2012

9.21 pm
Iphgenia Baal
where r u?

Facebook User
bondi beach

9.40 pm
Iphgenia Baal
just Googled it
lots of girls with sandy bums

9.43 pm
Facebook User
don't be jealous x

Iphgenia Baal
jealous? me?
i tried to call cos i wanted to say that i really took to heart what you said
so thank you for taking the time + talking so muchsense and being so
sweet tis v. rare other people's thoughts get through to me. XX

10.11 pm
Facebook User
Yes well......... it's only cos I know it and I've done it myself and I really
believe in learning from others mistakes there is nothing worse than
watching someone u care about fuck their shit up. u gotta learn some
tolerance because the way you go about things you get nothing and deep
down u know its just not worth it but hey, I'm happy u listened and hope
u are doing good...

10.53 pm

Iphgenia Baal

hello,

yes, but could say the same to you. in fact, is exactly what i WAS trying to say... but yes i'm an idiot and don't know what i'm talking about most of the time.. but that doesn't mean i'm not right sometimes. THAT'S ALL

i am going to africa next week.

dont be jealous ;) xxxx

Text
Sunday, 8 January 2012

6.13 pm
Iphgenia Baal
so i am quite enamoured with my new crush x

Facebook

Monday, 9 January 2012

Facebook User · 7.02 pm

just done my 3rd skydive this week !!!!!!! 7 more and they'll let me go by myself!! !!!!

78 PEOPLE like this

~~Josie Teller~~ · 7.05 pm

I have inspired you hehe!

~~Lester Lloyd~~ · 7.05 pm

jealous

~~Ben Fletcher~~ · 7.29 pm

killing it in Oz bruv. representin W4 down unda!!!

Facebook User · 7.17 pm

no i do not

2 PEOPLE like this

~~Rahim Siddiq~~ · 7.19 pm

do not what exactly fam

Facebook User · 7.25 pm

look below

~~Ahmed Mohid~~ · 7.32 pm

yes you do

Facebook User · 1.01 pm

wants a stiff cocking

14 PEOPLE like this

~~Jay Brown Lee~~ · 1.40 pm

slag

Facebook User · 7.14 pm

hot slag

~~Spencer Day~~ · 8.30 pm

loooooool Pillow Biter...! who FB raped you?

Facebook Messenger
Tuesday, 10 January 2012

8.04 pm
Iphgenia Baal
blanked by a skydiver in Oz
def one of my lowest moments
i'm embarrassed for everyone

8.09 pm
Facebook User
who is ur new crush??

Iphgenia Baal
YOU YOU IDIOT

Facebook User
hahahaaaaaaaaaa

8.12 pm
Iphgenia Baal
sucker

Facebook User
coolx

Facebook Messenger
Wednesday, 11 January 2012

4.01 pm
Facebook User
when did i blank you u cow?

4.04 pm
Iphgenia Baal
it was cross wires
i sent that days ago.

Facebook User
good.

Iphgenia Baal
stop being mean

Facebook User
i've lost my voice

Iphgenia Baal
cute
smoking fags?
or shouting at people?

Facebook User
not

4.05 pm
Iphgenia Baal
not cute?

Facebook User
yep
i have to whisper.
how u?

4.06 pm
Iphgenia Baal
i'm having the best time tho i kno u never believe me when i say that

Facebook User
oh really hahaaaaaa i went skydiving

Iphgenia Baal
i saw
made me feel sick !

4.07 pm
Facebook User
it was full on

Iphgenia Baal
i couldn't handle it
no way

Facebook User
u could

Iphgenia Baal
did u think u were gonna die?

4.08 pm
Facebook User
i always think i'm gonna die so yeah
not fun

Iphgenia Baal

what did you think before you jumped?

4.09 pm

Facebook User

i thought - this is weird i'm strapped to someone

4.12 pm

Iphgenia Baal

u r so romantic xxxxxxxxxxxxxx

Facebook
Thursday, 12 January 2012

Facebook User added a photo – with ~~Haw Thomas~~ · 5.15 pm

18 PEOPLE like this
~~Ty Wood~~ · 5.17 pm
yesssssssssssy
~~Ty Wood~~ · 5.18 pm
see u in a couple of days mate
~~Haw Thomas~~ · 5.20 pm
lets ditch him
~~Ty Wood~~ · 5.22 pm
hahahahahaha tye him to a tree

Iphgenia Baal · 6.07 pm
My most used swahili phrase this week has been 'wewe ni mbaguzi ubaguzo' ...
which means 'you are a racist fucker'
~~Emily Mosley~~, ~~Cole Alexander~~ and 22 OTHERS like this.
Iphgenia Baal · 6.10 pm
Usually followed by 'Nami kuchoma watoto wako'
Iphgenia Baal · 6.10 pm
which means I will burn your children :)
~~Pheobe Flynn Oliver~~ · 6.11 pm
bitching out across continents xxxx
~~Illi Garcia~~ · 7.04 pm
please be careful!!!!! we want you back in one peace

Facebook Messenger
Friday, 13 January 2012

2.21 am
Facebook User
i have no fear of death
it's just this constant annoyance in my head

2.22 am
Iphgenia Baal
where did that come from?

Facebook User
answer the question

Iphgenia Baal
it wasn't a question
but it would suit you more to stay alive

Facebook User
but i do have a slight death wish and it's not cos i'm unhappy
i cant quite work it out

2.23 am
Iphgenia Baal
i like talking about death on facebook
but i dunno

Facebook User
no u dont
nor do i

Iphgenia Baal
i think you've got close enough to the right idea
maybe slightly high risk strategy
but then i like high stakes

2.24 am
Facebook User
haaaaaaa

2.25 am
Iphgenia Baal
besides all i've ever wanted in life is a dead boyfriend

Facebook User
pahahahahaha
i'll see what i can do xx

Facebook Messenger
Saturday, 14 January 2012

5.10 am
Iphgenia Baal
don't think i miss u cos i don't.... x

5.17 am
Facebook User
listen just crack on

Iphgenia Baal
excuse me?

Facebook User
i'm a lost cause
trust me

Iphgenia Baal
don't make me hate you
please
i can't be bothered

Facebook User
listen
stop playing games with me
i know u r with someone
which is cool....
just would've been nice to hear it from you

5.18 am
Iphgenia Baal
excuse me?

119

5.19 am
Facebook User
don't feel like you have to bullshit me
i have a good source

Iphgenia Baal
you wish you could get out of it that easy
DROP DEAD

Facebook User
YOU wish u could get out of it THAT easy

5.20 am
Iphgenia Baal
why get in touch with me just to give me grief?
which good source?

Facebook User
i have friends
they tell me things...
besides all u do is give me grief

5.21 am
Iphgenia Baal
i bet they do
are these friends imaginary?

5.27 am
Facebook User
why u gotta be rude?
u gotta learn u can't control people all the time
i want to do whatever i want to do without having to answer to u
u can't hate me for me not thinking how u want me to think

5.30 am
Iphgenia Baal
and what exactly do you think I want you to think?
do i ask you where you are ? what you're fucking?
you try and dump me on facebook from the other side of the world and
expect me not to be pissed off?

Facebook User
don't try and be smart
you were the one saying 'i'll wait for you'
why bother?

5.32 am
Iphgenia Baal
oh what so you send me some msg saying 'crack on' whatever the fuck
that means

5.35 am
Facebook User
well?

5.37 am
Iphgenia Baal
i love u u big dummy!!!!

Facebook User
yes em

Iphgenia Baal
more to the point I AM IN AFRICA! and yes maybe I have spent the
last 2 nights trying to ignore hard ons pushed into the small of my back
without totally emasculating the owner standard grim shit that girls have
to tolerate daily AND while I realise u r on some party boy world tour its
been quite nice for me to be able to use you as an excuse to turn this idiot
down HAPPY?

eMail
Sunday, 22 January 2012

10.33 am
Iphgenia Baal
hello Facebook User,
i dunno if you even have anything to listen to songs on but either way...
i never DJ in London but in Africa i am FIRST SELECTA LADY BOSS
DJ and this was my No. 1 tune. playing off my crackberry or as all the
rastas call it, RUDEBOY PHONE. Made me think bout what you were
sayin about sending 2nd hand phones to Afreekah how access to information changes everything... well maybe u didn't say exactly that - i
paraphrase... thought perhaps i should try to do something... Obvs not
on the grand scale you could pull off, but still... EVERY RASTAMAN
SHOULD HAVE A CRACKBERRY!!
off to costa del crime tomorrow for a few weeks so don't get upset if you
can't find me when you get back
also, WHERE IS MY TUPAC SONG?
Jah Bless/Jobless.x
[Attachments: No-No-No_Bounty-Killah_&_Dawn_Penn.mp3]
[Photo24.jpg]

3.38 pm
Facebook User
honestly - my favourite thing is tan lines so.....there was the affection.
hope africa was all it lived up to be in ur head and will be looking for u
when i get home
u gonna be in marbella by any chance??
gonna be there in march for a week - puerta benus or however the fuck u
spell it xxxxxxxxxxxxx

3.39 pm
Iphgenia Baal
yes. that is exactly where i'm going... lots of rich cunts... stayin in san
pedro for a
couple of weeks. also, I've decided to dedicate my next book to you
because you are
the love of my life. x

4.03 pm
Facebook User
heyy,
my inbox wouldn't open for some reason
that all sounds very good
dedicate ur book to me?
not a funny joke
well, slightly funny xxxxx

Facebook

Tuesday, 24 January 2012

Iphgenia Baal > Facebook User · 8.15 am
Out of Africa. Gone Marbella. x

Facebook User commented on ~~Maria Duval~~'s post.

~~Maria Duval~~ · 4.14 pm
chanel couture show yesterday was beautiful #eco #zen #sexy well done
everyone and thanks to ~~Sarah Vallah~~ for getting my hair and make up
perfect and understanding how i wanted it. #fashion #savetheoceans
167 PEOPLE like this
~~Lia Tafari~~ · 5.00 pm
crew dem
~~Grace Well~~ · 9.03 pm
possee
~~Barry Hoyd~~ · 9.11 pm
Strictly boom tings
~~Gary Card~~ · 9.12 pm
y dnt we just dance!!! Lololol
Facebook User · 9.12 pm
yes yes
Facebook User · 9.12 pm
bell me. i'm in oz. will PM u my number
~~Dur Bol~~ · 9.14 pm
dats my girl
~~Jamie Gee~~ · 9.14 pm
you are SO beautiful
~~Juline Wiu~~ · 9.22 pm
stunning

Facebook Messenger
Tuesday, 24 January 2012

9.15 pm
Iphgenia Baal
don't ignore me pls
i can see u r online

Facebook Messenger
Wednesday, 25 January 2012

7.00 am

Iphgenia Baal

you pop up on my facebook more than any posh blonde, chat to every
ponyriding loser and ignore me.
NICE!

Text

Saturday, 28 January 2012

10.31 am

Iphgenia Baal

whatever then that was me being nice so ignore me to your detriment!

2.02 pm

actually fuck it... you are a bully.

it dun't cost nothing to be nice...

seems to me you aren't even boy enough to respect the women you fuck

so more of a misogynist than you think

you've got blood on your hands

greedy

delusional

i would hit you with a few more home truths, but I can't be bothered

Text
Sunday, 29 January 2012

11.11 pm
Facebook User
what are u on abou
if ur gonna be angry all the time can u just take it out on someone else
i'm having a really nice time where I am and really don't need this

11.12 pm
just stop x ·

Text
Monday, 30 January 2012

3.04 am
Iphgenia Baal
you can be sick of me if you like

3.05 am
i am drunk.

3.13 am
like u even give a shit

Facebook User
8.44 am
nutter
where r u?

9.14 am
oi.

9.48 am
Iphgenia Baal
on the run from kops and kunts

Facebook User
hope ur okay. x

eMail

Tuesday, 31 January, 2012

10.44 am
Iphgenia Baal
and delete me on facefuck. for what?
you need to start worrying about the consequences of your actions in the
real world and less how i make you look in front of friendships weighted
entirely on social media stats.

12.29 pm
Facebook User
a phone number is too much for u to handle
fb would make ur head explode
honestly try and give urself a break for a week or 2
and great u were in the pub all afternoon but i dont need to come out of
the cinema and have these rambling nonsensical messages on my phone
have a look at some of the shit you say to me
there is something seriously not right!!!!

Text
Wednesday, 1 February, 2012

10.12 am
Iphgenia Baal
apology not accepted then?

10.15 am
Facebook User
it's not a case of forgiven. it's a case of u need for ur own good to stop calling me
crazy and take a really good look at urself
i know it's hard but u dont like living like this

eMail
Thursday, 2 February 2012

7.19 am
Iphgenia Baal
what and ur life's so perfect is it? wanker

9.09 am
Facebook User
seems that way

eMail
Saturday, 4 February 2012

6.40 am
Iphgenia Baal
ur life is ridiculous. u follow these idiots round the world like some mindless puppy but don't you think if they really wanted you there they'd pay for your ticket instead of letting you go to such extreme lengths? To them, it's a game. One that ur losing!

10.07 am
Facebook User
is that what u do? tings?

Iphgenia Baal
power games = bullshit.

10.08 am
Facebook User
i only removed u because it pisses u off and i'm not likely to stop talking to 'posh blondes' as u call them anytime soon (happened to be someone ive known for 8 yrs and used to live with) BUT i hope you are having a good start to the year and keep on working if nothing else!!!!!!!!!!!!! xx

Iphgenia Baal
I said you popped up MORE than any given posh blonde, but misunderstand me all you like. The rest of the world does and it isn't cos I don't s p e l l i t o u t

10.12 am
Facebook User
i'm trying to make up with you cunt

Facebook
Saturday, 4 February 2012

Iphgenia Baal and **Facebook User** are now friends · 10.16 am

Iphgenia Baal · 10.13 am
i don't think i will ever get hitched, but if I was going to, this would def be 1st dance https://www.youtube.com/watch?v=JQCZkTD2Rh8

> **The Specials - Stupid Marriage**
> Artist: The Specials Song: Stupid Marriage
> Album: The Specials Year: 1979 KingLeon1daz
> 179,753 views. 2:28. youtube.com

Iphgenia Baal · 7.22 pm
i hate facebook

~~Zion Ana~~ · 7.47 pm
there is no darkness but ignorance

Iphgenia Baal · 10.15 am
https://www.youtube.com/results?search-query=tarhell+slim+you%re+go
nna+reap

> **Tarheel Slim & Little Ann - You're Gonna Reap
> (everything you sew)** Dance the modern dance/
> walk the modern walk/take that modern chance/
> /talk that modern talk... 2:35   youtube.com

Text
Sunday, 5 February 2012

4.43 am
Iphgenia Baal
life is weird. most romantic thing I heard today - don't remember the bad bits. Xxxxxxxxxxxx

4.45 am
Shiuldn't have sent last message. Prob'ly shouldn't send this one...but ...errrrrr.....

4.46 am
Shiuldn't have sent last message. Prob'ly shouldn't send this one...but ...errrrrr.....
Shiuldn't have sent last message. Prob'ly shouldn't send this one...but ...errrrrr.....

8.49 am
Facebook User
you're a good writer haha if nothing else, there's that.

8.51 am
Iphgenia Baal
we'll see

Facebook
Tuesday, 7 February 2012

12.42 am
Facebook User
also if you are still interested i think i have worked out i am
interested in everything and committed to nothing
still haven't worked out if thats good or bad

12.43 am
Iphgenia Baal
i think you just like the sound of that. even from just watching and not
getting any myself (HA) it is obvious you are one of the most loyal souls
around. maybe why you are so guarded...

Facebook User
maybe but it takes years

Iphgenia Baal
to be a cunt?

12.44 am
Facebook User
for me to give a shit

Iphgenia Baal
either way great

12.47 am
Facebook User
yeah

eMail
Tuesday, 14 February 2012

3.38 pm
Iphgenia Baal
much as I've always believed that it's ok to be a slut for a big dick, I think
I decided that I can't let myself be treated so dismissively: i'm out

5.03 pm
Facebook User
slag is right
how many?

5.07 pm
Iphgenia Baal
2 many men 2 many many men

8.15 pm
unless u rnt joking in which case GET FUCKED

eMail
Thursday, 16 February 2012

6.33 pm

Iphgenia Baal

someone asked me last night what went down between me + u, saying how u'd been banging on about how amazing i was for years, i tried to be as honest, saying how we had a little thing and then u bailed and i schitzed. someone overheard. their reaction, "Facebook User primordial dwarf? king of the mushrooms." To quote you PAHAHAHAHAHAHA

6.44 pm

Facebook User

if u hate me so much, why u wanna chat to me all the time?

6.58 pm

Iphgenia Baal

I don't hate you. I just don't get why u wanna trash this. It's such a shame! Besides, it's not even me that your running from x

7.07 pm

Facebook User

Listen. I've said this a million times. And the fact that I'm willing to say it again should prove to you that I do care. It's just that I don't know what is going on in my life and I don't want to lead you on so much as I want to say yeah cool to everything, I'm trying not to be a dick. You don't make it easy though! X

Facebook Messenger
Sunday, 19 February 2012

4.34 pm
Iphgenia Baal
do u know when u r gonna be back?

4.39 pm
Facebook User
going thailand
back in march but not gonna be around much
leaving again soon xx

4.51 pm
Iphgenia Baal
u going marbella?

4.54 pm
Facebook User
dar

Iphgenia Baal
r u telling me i won't see u?

Facebook User
es salaam
tanzania

4.55 pm
Iphgenia Baal
yes i know where it is

Facebook User
got a job maybe
motors
import and export bebe

4.58 pm
Iphgenia Baal
ha!
u best be nervous coming through customs bruv I'm TELLIN u

5.08 pm
Facebook User
what does that mean?
what does that mean?

5.09 pm
Iphgenia Baal
it means fuck U

Google
Sunday, 19 February 2012

cars imports drugs tanzania
About 137,000 results (0.52 seconds)

Export to Tanzania
Ad www.exportingisgreat.gov.uk/Tanzania
Forced to commit a crime and sentenced to death? Donate now!
Opportunities · Support · Become an Exporter

Interpol closes in on drug trafficking in East Africa
www.theeastafrican.co.ke/news/-/2558/1017972//index.html
27 Sep 2010 - An extensive Interpol operation is underway to halve international
motor vehicle theft linked to the drug trade... LEGISLATIONS ON IM-
PORTS... Anti-Money Laundering Groups are some of the biggest drug trans-
portations being smuggled across land... Tanzania, Sudan, Ethiopia...

[PDF] Illicit Dealings: International Organized Crime - cnpds
www.cnpds.it/documenti/fb95a6fd7f209916197336323df897de.pdf
Cannabis and khat trafficking between 2001 to 2004 showed fairly... illicit
trafficking IN FIREARMS is a major concern... theft 786 Aggravated theft
30,556 Breaking & entering 23,415 Motor vehicle theft 223 Counterfeit
currency 398 Drug offenses 4,069

Trading across borders - Tanzania Investment Centre
www.tic.co.tz/menu/287?l=en

Searches related to cars imports drugs tanzania

importing cars to tanzania regulations	drug dealers in tanzania
cost of shipping a car from uk to tanzania	used cars tanzania
tanzania car dealers	drug lords in tanzania

Google
Sunday, 19 February 2012

drug dealing sentences
About 433,000 results (0.51 seconds)

Crimestoppers: The only independent UK crime fighting charity
Ad https://crimestoppers-uk.org/ 0800 555111
Can't Go To The Police? You Can Report Crime Anonymously Nobody
Will Know Who You Are. Crimestoppers Trust is a partnership between
the police, the media and the community to fight crime.
Give Information - Most Wanted - Keeping Safe - Donate

Give Information Online
... be made of your information, or
can fill out our anonymous ...

Most Wanted
Crimestoppers posts the Most
Wanted by Region, County ...

Drugs penalties - GOV.UK
https://www.gov.uk/penalties-drug-possession-dealing
12 Aug 2011 - The penalties - drug classification, fines and sentences... Crack
cocaine, ecstasy (MDMA), heroin, LSD, magic mushrooms, methadone,
methamphetamine Possession 7 years in prison Supply Up to life in prison...

The Dope on Drug Sentencing
www.dailymail.co.uk/heroindealers-escape-jail-new-sentencing-proposals
19 Feb 2012 - Under mind boggling new proposals, dealer could supply
more than 900 hits of heroin and still escape jail. (Posed by model) ... For
example, say this was 2kg of heroin (a Class A drug), or other methyl-
phenidate substances future drug dealers

[PDF] Drug offences: Public consultation (easy read version part 3)
https://www.sentencingcouncil.org.uk/Get_Off_Drugs
by J Jacobson - 2011 - Cited by 7 - Related articles

Crimestoppers

Monday, 20 February 2012

What is the crime or incident you would like to tell us about?

Arson Assault Burglary Business Crime Criminal Damage Cybercrime
Drink-driving Drug manufacture **Drug Trafficking** Environmental
Crime Fraud Fugitive Campaign Handing Stolen Goods Human
Trafficking Illegal Tobacco Immigration Most Wanted Murder Possesion
of weapons Proceeds of Crime Rape Robbery Smuggling Tax evasion
Terrorism, Theft Vehicle Crime

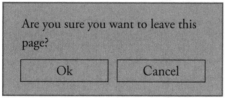

Are you sure you want to leave this page?

| Ok | Cancel |

Do you know it happened?
    ☒ yes ☒ no
When did it happen?
    __ / __ / ____
Do you know who the offender is?
    ☒ yes ☒ no
Were there any weapons involved?
    ☒ yes ☒ no
Please can you describe the criminal activity / incident / person(s)?

Do you know the name of the person involved?
    ☒ yes ☒ no
What was the name of the person involved?

Crimestoppers is a Registered Company No. 5382856. Charity No. 1108687 Address: Crimestoppers, PO Box 324, Wallington SM6 6BG

Crimestoppers   Contact us   Media Centre   Privacy Policy   Newsletter   Other Languages   Ts&Cs   Sitemap

Facebook Messenger
Tuesday, 22 February 2012

7.12 am
Iphgenia Baal
I'm really gonna enjoy watching you get fat and old x

7.14 am
Facebook User
u and ur weird behaviour just makes me pity u

7.18 am
Iphgenia Baal
hahah
ditto

7.21 am
Facebook User
and ur constant want for some attention is sad
i'm sorry I have a life
i'm sorry I don't want to see someone who is a complete spoilt brat.

7.22 am
Iphgenia Baal
"soooooooo fit"

7.23 am
Facebook User
who u? that's ur problem
delusional
ur not nice to be around

Iphgenia Baal
nice try primordial

7.24 am
Facebook User
really weird

7.25 am
why don't you go pick on milo?
he likes it.

7.27 am
Iphgenia Baal
u r my new inspiration!

7.30 am
Facebook User
and what are you ?

7.31 am
Iphgenia Baal
a honeytrap for arrogant pricks

Facebook User
pffff
yeah right.

Facebook Messenger
Friday, 25 February 2012

11.26 am
Iphgenia Baal
you know what the shittest thing about all this is is that the only thing that
made us hooking up not pathetic and insane - pop op - was the fact that
it was real. not just casual socialite shag
i was upfront with you from the start
now i just feel a fool for falling for it cos I totally did
funny I guess
ha ha
NOT

eMail
Monday, 28 February 2012

8.28 am

Iphgenia Baal

besides, interest without commitment will get you exactly nowhere. you bang on about how emma is so selfish, but from where i'm standing you're not so different....there is no one with the bollox to match their front in the circle of people u know. you were the only possibility i'd spotted so far and even you've come up short... always looking for quick-fix rather than proper solution. see something you don't like, ignore it. but do you ever stop and ask yourself where the true cost of the way you (and we all, to some extent) live actually falls? On whose shoulders?

One of the reasons people start relationships based on trust is so they can fuck each other properly. u r problem is that you're still scared of vaginas. can't look one in the eye, forget about take your clothes off in front of it. excuse me if i sound angry, it's not at you...IT'S AT THE ENTIRE PUMPED UP MACHO DICKHEAD POPULATION WHO ARE FUCKING EVERYTHING UP FOR EVERYONE, and not getting close to what they or anyone else is actually after.

i have plenty of dickheads i could get into something with but i started this with you so much as i hear what you are saying about wanting to do what you want and not having to answer to me/anyone... having respect for someone does not differ to having respect for urself.

Facebook

Tuesday, 29 February 2012

Facebook User · 11.56 am

gonna miss a lot of things about Thailand, but U PAY NOW won't be one of them

22 PEOPLE like this

~~Robbin Banks~~ · 11.57 am

when u bk mannnn u been gone 4 ages now u nomad ?

~~Delmas Malakoual~~ · 12.12 pm

:D same same!

~~Charlotte Hayes-Jones~~ · 12.51 pm

SAME SAME BUT DIFFERENT - hahahahahaha miss you benny xx

~~Ellie Bell~~ · 1.01 pm

Hahahaha epic

~~Camilla Hermansen~~ · 1.09 pm

All that bullshit's for the birds, you ain't nothin' but av vulture

~~Ed Poulter~~ · 2.43 pm

Mate, any chance you can bring me back some Valium please?!

~~Stefan Rowno-Gowno Pierrearia~~ · 2.43 pm

But chicks with Dicks will be mised sorely.

Facebook User · 3.44 pm

Sorry eddie boy already in KL - I have about 20 - u can have 10

~~Martin Offiah~~ · 5.00 pm

Have you been cheating on Jack with Ladyboys again lol

~~Ed Poulter~~ · 6.35 pm

You star! Thanks dude!

~~Moni Mon~~ · 6.42 pm

Pay me!!!!

Facebook User · 9.17 pm

Martin - if I didn't jack would only think I was soft

Facebook User · 10.43 pm

Moni - u gave my children away and they died through neglect

eMail

Tuesday, 29 February 2012

3.33 am

Facebook User

dont worry – im fully aware of all the bad i do having consequences.
i just dislocated my shoulder in my sleep. if thats not karma then fuck.
you really need to chill out with your lectures to me however. the funny
thing is you reckon you're so good at reading it all but you get it so wrong
every time.

Emma didn't owe me anything so I don't know why you are bothered and
the only one scared out here is you - scared and lonely and attempting
to replace the fear inside you with anger and malevolence, I've seen weak
people do it a thousand times over and I can see it so clearly it's painful.
Everything good in your life you seem to fuck up with this bullshit at-
titude, learn to be humble and chill the fuck out – you will achieve more.
As for me I'm comfortable with how I am and don't need a lecture EVER
from you nor do I need to send others lectures but this is the fourth or fifth
time I've experienced a tirade of garbage from you for no reason. Under-
neath it all you're a fucking cool, intelligent girl – just stop the bullshit
front and learn that people do what the fuck they want – this is life. I'm
not scared of having relationships or people I fully trust but the fewer the
better.

Try and figure yourself out before you go talking about shit you know
nothing, and I mean nothing about.

I don't need or want a response to this.

eMail
Thursday, 3 March 2012

10.29 am
Iphgenia Baal
i am sorry for the aggro. not meant as a lecture... just ideas about things.
i'm happy to be wrong. just hope you know me well enough by now to
realise that i don't mean any harm by it. in fact, the opposite.
you know I'd love to see you, but since I've been such an idiot I will leave
any making arrangements up to you.
no more rubbish, i promise xx

Facebook
Friday, 4 March 2012

Iphgenia Baal updated her cover photo · 4.23 pm

note to self written by a man with chronic amnesia and a one-liner from his girl

now i am ~~TOTALLY~~ perfectly awake (1st TIME)
now i <u>am</u> ~~CERTAINLY~~ perfectly awake (1st TIME)
now i <u>am</u> ~~REALLY~~ perfectly awake (1st TIME)
now i <u>am</u> ~~ALMOST~~ perfectly awake (1st TIME)
now i <u>am</u> perfectly awake (1st TIME)
now i <u>am</u> <u>REALLY</u> awake (1st TIME)
food arrived - a delicious piece of chocolate
1st patience games ends - now I am really awake
Hallo Darling! I love you! x x x
I am completely awake - <u>first time</u>, but i can't
Darling goes home just as i wake up completely
" delivers a lovely apple - <u>now</u> I am truly

7 PEOPLE like this

~~Sasha Banks~~ · 4.44 pm

god i dream of a life like this

~~Sasha Banks~~ · 4.44 pm

born to forget

Facebook User · 3.13 pm

big choon https://www.youtube.com/watch?v=3QjcA3FuWO4

Cocoa Tea – Girl Go Home (18 & Over) One of my all time fav's from the 80's digital era ... Your browser does not currently recognize any of the video formats available. Click here to visit our ...

43 PEOPLE like this

eMail
Saturday, 5 March 2012

5.38 pm
Iphgenia Baal
i guess that's a blank then. probs my fault for being part-time bunny
boiler etc.
i'm not as bad as i seem

6.02 pm
actually, i probably am

6.18 pm
but since i seem intent on going all out and making a fool of myself...
there was this one time, i think the first time i came to yours, and you
pinned down on the bed and said 'i wanna see how long i can stay still inside you for' but you couldn't stay still and i said that that was my game.
that millisecond is why i get like this about you. it was proper and is all i
am after xxxx

Facebook
Sunday, 6 March 2012

Iphgenia Baal · 4.51 pm
First they ignore you, then they laugh and ridicule you, then they attack you and want to burn you. And then they build monuments to you. And that is exactly what is going to happen.
10 PEOPLE like this
Iphgenia Baal · 5.02 pm
phase one is going well
~~Paul Halloran~~ · 5.07 pm
good stuff!
Iphgenia Baal · 5.09 pm
a quote wrongly attributed to mahatma ghandi
Iphgenia Baal · 5.10 pm
was in fact was a trade union leader in a speech in 1914
Iphgenia Baal · 5.10 pm
Nicholas Klein
~~Harri Watson~~ · 5.11 pm
still works
~~Angela Warner~~ · 5.11 pm
ghandi was overrated
~~Angela Warner~~ · 5.14 pm
anyway wasn't he posh? hahahaa
~~Harri Watson~~ · 5.47 pm
in the age of misinformation you've got to take what you can get
~~Mykola Xanthe Kryonky Baal~~ · 5.59 pm
whose got the petrol?

eMail
Sunday, 6 March 2012

10.04 pm

Facebook User

listen u mad, impatient girl

3 days ago u said u will leave it to me and u have lasted long haven't u?

10.07 pm

i'm not a creative outlet for u either so put ur writing skills into something positive x

11.41 pm

Iphgenia Baal

ok ok ur right, i'm sorry

half on it xx

11.49 pm

Iphgenia Baal

strollin past chicken cottage in kentish town, almost called but then thought i would probably call just as you landed and would look like some psycho stalker xxxx

Attachment: chicken-cottage.jpg

Facebook Messenger
Wednesday, 9 March 2012

10.40 am
Iphgenia Baal
soooo... are you are back? x

4.30 pm
Facebook User
yes
how r u?x

Iphgenia Baal
i am scared to see you!
don't want it to kick off xx

4.43 pm
Facebook User
it'll only kick off cos of ur stupid behavioural problems

4.47 pm
Iphgenia Baal
u should just learn to enjoy it ;) x

5.00 pm
Facebook User
please learn that i will never enjoy it
i take conflict extremely seriously

Facebook
Saturday, 12 March 2012

Facebook User shared a <u>link</u> · 9.14 pm
https://www.youtube.com/watch?v=EiBgcrYe8G8

Curren$y – Jet Life (Stoned Immaculate)
Intro: [Don't miss this jet ho] [x4] Talking jet life to the next life] ... Girls follow, recognize and seek guidance on counting dollars / High on top a money mountain, never coming down it [4.26] YOUTUBE.COM

11 PEOPLE like this

~~Chelsea Leyland~~ uploaded a new photo to the album BDL massssiiiiiive - with **Facebook User** and 6 others · 3.13 pm

40 PEOPLE like this

~~Liz Tafari~~ · 3.50 pm
that face cracks me up

~~Alice Palm Tree~~ · 3.51 pm
yes yes

~~Naimh Soto~~ · 3.57 pm
love you bro

Facebook User · 9.52 pm
niggas in the point aint changed

Facebook Messenger
Saturday, 12 March 2012

1.37 am

Iphgenia Baal

i'm visualising a reality show about Bedales brats a la Made In Chelsea, avec toi to appeal to the faux rudeboy contingent.

Facebook Messenger
Monday, 14 March 2012

2.34 am
Facebook User
it seems like you do a lot bothering me so much

10.39 am
Iphgenia Baal
finally a response!

10.40 am
Facebook User
learn some patience and chill i am sooooo fucking stressed got nowhere
to live and no money have so much on my plate right now u would have
a heart attack and die if confronted by it and then I have to listen to this
shit you are pouring in my ear? come on

Iphgenia Baal
i love it when you tell me off!
why do u have nowhere to live?
plus I know you aren't broke off shore bank accounts? ha

10.53 am
hello? don't ignore me please

10.58 am
fine then forget it! PRICK as usual! u need to learn how to have a proper
conversation, as in GET OVER URSELF

2.07 am
Facebook User
if I had the time I would lock you in a cupboard and teach you patience.

Facebook Messenger
Saturday, 19 March 2012

1.22 am
Iphgenia Baal
A lead would suit you but not as much as a cage.

1.43 am
Facebook User
ur mum

Iphgenia Baal
ur fucking mum u twat

1.48 am
Facebook User
u got issues real delusional problems see u one day or maybe not! loser

1.50 am
Iphgenia Baal
you would love to love me sadly, totally incapableand no you won't see
me but you'll hear of me. thankfully it'll all be socialite gossip, largely
uninformed and rooted in fear. but then you know all about that right?
currently a victim of it urself. everyone's got something to say!
either way, I'm looking forward to your next 'episode'. psycho. why did u
glass that guy anyway? I heard he was just trying to help. says it all really.

Facebook User
don't u get it I'm not interested. shit way of trying to speak to me and me
not fancying u anymore is not me being mean. it's just reality.

Iphgenia Baal
who cares?

Text
Sunday, 20 March 2012

2.00 am
Iphgenia Baal
You have no idea what I am about. My disguise is perfected to a T(wat).
Sadly for you, you can't tell the difference between what is and isn't. Which
works for me! It really doesn't matter what people think, and it matters even
less what they say. What matters is what is. But u r far too wrapped up in I
don't know what to figure that.
Cos I didn't like fucking you that much. I only liked how much you liked
fucking me. You can deny it all you want, but we were both there. And I
was sober hahaha cos I can deal

2.01 am
Ruthless + spineless = weird combination

2.02 am
As is a total lack of conscience with being a needy twat. Uh, just hold me.

7.09 am
What i don't get is that you are obsessed with the fact that I am trying to
control you when I can (clearly) barely control myself!

Text
Tuesday, 22 March 2012

7.16 am

Iphgenia Baal

altho for the record, I've never really minded anything you've done. I think you are an amazing boy. And still will... So you can do with that what you will...which is probably trash it, but that's your move.

7.31 am

besides - i think you will find in the long run that an honest life has a much lower price than any easy one.

7.46 am

you spend your whole time dicklicking a bunch of arrogant toffs who are not only stupid but ugly to boot... 5 mins listening to their vile spew actually makes heroin addiction/suicide seem like a viable alternative

Text
Wednesday, 23 March 2012

3.54 am
Iphgenia Baal
and i'm not stupid either, you pretend to be one sort of person to me, but you talk to other people in a totally different way.

Text
Thursday, 24 March 2012

4.00 pm

Iphgenia Baal

you are a control freak who can only really communicate through social media because you are too scared to do it face to face. i mean look what happened last time! a joke. stop trying to be something you are not.

4.19 pm

you are too clever and too stupid for the world you live in so make a choice before the whole thing blows up in your face.

4.22 pm

and no, that is not a threat.

Text
Friday, 25 March 2012

7.27 am
Iphgenia Baal
you are totally selfish. i have been trying to speak with you properly for
days. not on stupid phone or facefuck. all that shit is bollocks.

7.29 am
you are clearly too scared to engage with reality in any form it takes.
everything is one big joke, pretending to be some sort of small time G.
people like you make this world worse. the kind of guy who builds houses
in 3rd world countries prone to earthquakes, knowing they are going to
collapse. i should shop you to the cops but it's not even worth it.

7.33 am
sad thing is that usually when i get treated as badly as this by someone i
feel the need to act - get them evicted, arrested, into a fight - but in your
case, you do it to yourself. it's too easy.

8.06 am
your whole life is a stalemate. no one is allowed to speak their mind, or
say anything about anything. just a bitchy playground clique. you
honestly think a single one of them give a fuck about you?

Text
Thursday, 31 March 2012

11.00 am

Iphgenia Baal

congratulations on not being dead aka happy birthday xx
[paperclip: IMG0000034.JPG]

1.46 am

Facebook User

nutta x

Text
Saturday, 2 April 2012

7.07 pm
Iphgenia Baal
i just spent two hours brushing the knots out of my hair.
made me think of you s

8.08 pm
Facebook User
i can't wait to mess with your hair xxxx

Text
Wednesday, 6 April 2012

8.33 am
Iphgenia Baal
why leave like that?
u didn't even kiss me goodbye?

8.40 am
Facebook User
who says i didn't?

8.44 am
Iphgenia Baal
u just disappeared. it's mean.

8.46 am
Facebook User
shit to do luv xxx

Iphgenia Baal
ur skin is grey
u look like ur on ur last legs
u obviously feel guilty as shit for whatever uve been up to
why not try and SORT IT OUT????

2.42 pm
Facebook User
do u ever let anything go?
we had a nice time x

Facebook
Thursday, 7 April, 2012

Facebook User · 6.09 pm
LOST MY PHONE - NUMBERS AND PINS XX
7 PEOPLE like this
~~Charlotte Chamberlin Taylor~~ · 6.09 pm
This somehow doesn't surprise me after last night!
Facebook User · 7.07 pm
eaxacto - u missed out big time
~~India Bell~~ · 7.14 pm
hahaaa yeah yeah im coming next weekend !
~~Alexia Niedzielski~~ · 7.21 pm
ahahah so last night was pretty intense!
~~Charlotte Chamberlin Taylor~~ · 7.26 pm
the floor was his and he was anybody's
~~Tamara Is Cool~~ · 9.33 pm
2810166C xxx
~~Bilal Mann~~ · 9.35 pm
idiot !!!
~~Deah Bow Dewawa~~ · 9.41 pm
07500123197 283a9eeb x
~~Ods Ward~~ · 10.25 pm
004797638353
Facebook User · 10.49 pm
charlotte- that is so mean - there was at least 1% not up for it

Text
Friday, 8 April 2012

3.01 pm
Iphgenia Baal
actually i think maybe a girl who can't speak English might be the way forward for you. I mean eventually she will bail but...

10.02 pm
Facebook User
seriously WHAT DO YOU WANT?

10.03 pm
Iphgenia Baal
to be a nutter that you regret

10.04 pm
Facebook User
no really
i'm asking
maybe i can help you

10.05 pm
Iphgenia Baal
for you to fuck me like you hate me

10.07 pm
Facebook User
such a bitch

Facebook
Tuesday, 12 April 2012

Facebook User was tagged in 3 pictures in ~~Lui Tafari~~'s album · 8.52 pm

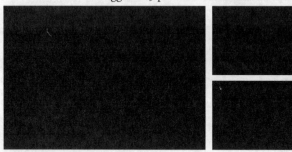

22 PEOPLE like this

~~Ben Hypolite~~ · 8.52 pm
where it all began

~~Luis Attawalpa Attawalpa~~ · 8.55 pm
i'm glad there's not a pic of us from the end

~~Danny Brady~~ · 9.12 pm
there is!

~~Maria Duval~~ · 9.12 pm
BOOOOOM!!!!

~~Maria Duval~~ · 9.13 pm
yes boys!!!!

~~Ben Hypolite~~ · 9.16 pm
Noushy, you're hair

~~Lui Tafari~~ · 9.22 pm ~~Ben Hypolite~~
cuties

~~Ty Wood~~ · 9.39 pm
mate you already looked wrecked

~~Henry Men~~ · 9.37 pm
 YOUR A WEIRDO WHO HAS SPLIT PERSONALITIES/MILD
SCHIZOPHRENIA, ONES A KILLER AND THE OTHERS JUST
CHAOS HAHA

eMail

Wednesday, 13 April 2012

11.30 am

Iphgenia Baal

Hello, have you changed your number? I tried to call. X

5.55 pm

Well BLAH how boring. If all you wanted was some dimwit blonde, then why even go for me in the first place?

eMail
Thursday, 14 April 2012

11.12 am
Iphgenia Baal

oh whatever, i dunno why i play this stupid role.... i thought this was
gonna be nice, but already, it isn't. i can take the blame or put it on you...
makes no difference. i understand both positions and why people react
the way they do but in reality this situation is exactly what i was trying
to avoid. you feeling aggrieved and me feeling fucked over ... neither of
which needs to be the case... it's just how these things go.
ephemeral nothing bullshit.
not that you need telling.
i dunno what to make of the things u say. its like ur 2 different people +
yes i am aware that u said that to me. doesn't mean it isn't true to u too.
what i do know is that once you have fucked someone, you should never
ever speak to them over the internet. facebook=death.
anyway, i still hope this is gonna turn out nice. i have an inkling that if
we hang out, it'll be fine, but maybe that won't happen again after last
time. not like i can force it... but please know that i am trying to be good.
good to you if nothing else.
that's all.
i do believe boys should protect the girls they fuck, and stand up for them
etc etc even though that almost never happens... which is a shame,
because it means the best girls end up crazed and abused and no good for
no one.
r u getting me?

Facebook
Sunday, 17 April 2012

Facebook User · 7.09 pm
LOST MY PHONE AGAIN - DONT ASK .... NUMBERS AND
PINS XX
3 PEOPLE like this
~~Victoria Hjeldstadh~~ · 7.10 pm
omg
~~Deah Bow Dewawa~~ · 7.12 pm
Are you kidding?
~~Deah Bow Dewawa~~ · 7.13 pm
07500123197 txt your pin xx
~~Tamara IsCool~~ · 7.43 pm
cant you just look at the last status?
Facebook User · 8.25 pm
good point Tamara
~~Abbey Woods~~ · 11.26 pm
Your just like me always loosing phones
~~Abbey Woods~~ · 11.26 pm
add me benny 281E5237

Iphgenia Baal <u>via</u> My Most Used Words · 11.12 pm
needs open mind
My most used words

Needs: Used 113 times
Open: Used 102 times
Mind: Used 89 times
...See More

2 PEOPLE like this

eMail
Monday, 18 April 2012

6.20 pm

Iphgenia Baal

The more I realise your group of friends, the more freaked out I get - this faux camaraderie based on what I don't know, money, fashiony, face-booky, hysterically, druggy bollocks, where what - one person is allowed and another isn't? Of course there are some of you that are real, but they are not only the exceptions but come complete with this terrifying clique who operate like some sort of succubus. The type of people who enjoy it when someone they know is fucking up, will dance around a graveside as long as there's someone taking photos. You said yourself that I say nasty shit to people as a way of showing love for them but maybe it is more straightforward than that. Maybe I just tell the truth and people don't like it. NO ONE these days is willing to take ANY criticism. Doubt the consensus and it's like the middle fucking ages. BURN THE WITCH. When in truth everything that is, isn't. People only say stunning under-neath pictures of ugly girls - like some weird inverse bullying – egging people onwho won't get far.

6.22 pm

There is no such thing as an innocent bystander and all diplomats are only in it for themselves.

Facebook

Thursday, 21 April 2012

~~Eric Thorp~~ > **Iphgenia Baal** · 7.32 pm

JFSJ

3 PEOPLE likes this

Iphgenia Baal · 7.40 pm

it's gonna catch on

~~Eric Thorp~~ · 7.42 pm

was fun vomming and smoking crack with you this weekend

~~Eric Thorp~~ · 7.45 pm

fucking three people have asked me if we were really smoking crack

Iphgenia Baal · 7.47 pm

suicide pact? might as well organise it publicly, avoid speculation

~~Eric Thorp~~ · 7.50 pm

lets go out in a blaze of vomit and crack smoke xxxx

Iphgenia Baal · 7.50 pm

i'm gassing myself in a zipcar

Iphgenia Baal changed her cover photo · 10.06 pm

GROWTH IS SHIT

JOBS ARE SHIT

ALL I WANT IS REVENGE

15 PEOPLE like this

~~Phoebe Flynn Oliver~~ · 10.12 pm

WANT!!! where is this from????

Iphgenia Baal · 10.12 pm

poster. will get u one xxxxx

Text
Sunday, 24 April 2012

7.22 am
Facebook User
U Chilled out yet?

Iphgenia Baal
had an orgasm now so yeah

Facebook User
who's the lucky guy?

Iphgenia Baal
prettydumblightskin
i think you went to school together.

7.23 am
Facebook User
u don't kno any black people I kno
ur problem is u argue all the time
boring
good luck with ur orgasms

7.27 am
plus everyone knows there are no black people in Chiswick hahaa
anyway nice talking to you have more important things to get back to x

Iphgenia Baal
like sucking up to posh kids trying to get a hitch?

Facebook User
What's a hitch?

Iphgenia Baal

heathrow airport to pick up some smack, then the movies, right?

a ride loser

can't wait for someone to open your eyes

token yokel haha

usually poshos pick someone with some talent but in ur case selling drugs

will do

ttragic!

7.35 am

Facebook User

i love ur delusional world I live in

u r peculiar

u catch feelings, I catch flights. only thing I do at Heathrow

7.37 am

and what poshos?

Iphgenia Baal

oh you so give a shit! hilarious!

Facebook User

the poorest little rich girl out of them all

pissed cos ur family is rich

7.39 am

Iphgenia Baal

errrrrr yeah i am distraught

your comebacks really ain't what they used to be

losing ur touch?

Facebook User

just got no need to impress you anymore.

got what i wanted hahaha

don't call me

Craigslist
Wednesday, 27 April 2012

Post to Classifieds
  CL london, UK > personals > choose category:

- ☒ personal/romance
- ☒ dating (long-term relationship)
- ☒ missed connection
- ☒ casual encounter (no strings attached)
- ☒ strictly platonic (non-romantic, non-sexual, just friends)

Users must comply with all applicable laws, the CL terms of use, and all posted site rules.

By posting you confirm you are 18 or older. If we believe you impersonated someone, or posted their information, you authorise release of your information to the victim, and agree to pay $1,000 or actual damages, whichever is greater.

vw8hh-3913339384@pers.craigslist

Poor Little Rich Girl Looking 4 Fun
Location: London

4 REAL: Just been kicked out of boarding school and been grounded. I am sooooooo bored! Any hot older guys out there with any ideas about how to get revenge on my horrible daddy, text me!!!!!! 07854 224 443.

it's NOT ok to contact this poster with services or other commercial interests
posting ID: 3913339384
posted: 2012-04-27, 10:04am BST

© craigslistCL help   safety   privacy feedback terms about

Facebook Messenger
Wednesday, 27 April 2012

7.18 am
Facebook User
are you out of ur fucking mind?
take it down
take it down
take it down
take it down now
what the fuck are you playing at?

8.08 am
Iphgenia Baal
i just wanted you to know what it feels like to be treated like a cunt just because you've got one

You cannot reply to this thread

Facebook
Saturday, 30 April 2012

Iphgenia Baal changed her profile picture · 10.06 am
thinking of getting some t shirts printed up

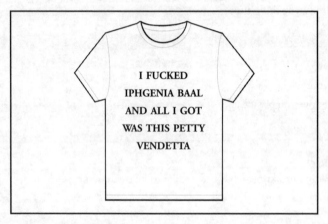

13 PEOPLE like this
~~Phoebe Flynn Oliver~~ · 10.09 am
get me one pleeeeeease
~~Anita Crupper~~ · 10.14 am
hello "force to be reckoned with" how are things working out since the
fiasco the other day?
Iphgenia Baal · 10.15 am
fine, since i remembered i don't give a shit
~~Anita Crupper~~ · 10.17 am
yeah right you don't
~~Kevin What~~ · 10.22 am
this is the greatest thing ever
~~Miriam Montague~~ · 10.23 am
NEED

eMail
Sunday, 1 May 2012

5.55 pm

Iphgenia Baal

You can block me on facefuck and change your number and probably delete this email without even reading it, but what you FAIL to realise is the one FLAW in your INTOLERANT attempt to silence me, which is that IN REALITY I STILL EXIST!!!!

I am STILL walking around breathing and thinking and talking—mostly about YOU hahahahaha

eMail
Friday, 6 May 2012

1.30 pm
Iphgenia Baal
Dear Facebook User,
It goes without saying that I am sorry for giving your number to loads of pervs. You didn't deserve it.
I know I can be an irrational nitwit sometimes — I guess I just find it hard to get a grip BUT I am writing you this email to let you know that I've got one now.
If you don't want to talk to me anymore then I understand, but I'd still like to talk to you

xx

eMail

Tuesday, 12 May 2012

5.15 pm

Iphgenia Baal

all I am trying to say is WE SHOULD BE FRIENDS! x

Facebook
Thursday, 12 May 2012

Iphgenia Baal updated her profile picture · 8.21 am

15 PEOPLE like this
~~Cole Alexander~~ · 11.42 am
i like a hot mess
Iphgenia Baal · 11.47 am
u think u do
~~Camilla Green~~ · 1.12 pm
<3 sid

Iphgenia Baal · 8.15 am
"disgust always bears the imprint of desire." PA & AW
12 PEOPLE like this
~~Rhiannon Hughes~~ · 10.02 am
who are PA and AW?
Iphgenia Baal · 10.10 am
got it from https://www.jstor.org/stable/25067359?seq=1#
Iphgenia Baal · 10.11 am
aka i dunno

eMail

Friday, 20 May 2012

2.15 pm

Iphgenia Baal

YAH YAH I get the message – you hate my guts.

Google
Saturday, 21 May 2012

Facebook User
About 162,000,000 results (1.06 seconds)

Facebook User Profiles | Facebook
https://en-gb.facebook.com/public/Ben-Thomas
View the profiles of people named Facebook User.

Facebook User - School of Arts - University of Kent
https://www.kent.ac.uk/arts/staff-profiles/hpa/thomas.html
Facebook User. History of Art and Media - Senior Lecturer. B.D.H. FacebookUser@kent.ac.uk; 01227 823403.

Some results may have been removed under data protection law in Europe.

Searches related to Facebook User

Facebook User chroma

Facebook User photographer

Facebook User death

Facebook User facebook

Text
Thursday, 26 May 2012

11.11 pm
Iphgenia Baal
i recently realised that all the shit we sling at each other is really only
aimed at ourselves x

11.13 pm
Facebook User
ur weird and lonely and sad and old
ur not a nutter, just a rejected poor soul
sorry I can't help u x

11.15 pm
Iphgenia Baal
don't worry about it x

Google
Thursday, 26 May 2012

how to hack facebook
About 94,600,000 results (0.66 seconds)

Unofficial: Facebook Hack Online For Free
https://www.facebook.com/the.facebook.hack.online.free/answers you are
on the right track! In the next few minutes you will be able to hack ANY Facebook account (Your girlfriend/boyfriend's account, your children' accounts)
how to hack my boyfriend's facebook account? 20 Aug 2011
should I hack my boyfriend's facebook? 21 Feb 2011

4 Ways to Crack a Facebook Password and How to Protect Your ID
null-byte.wonderhowto.com/4-ways-crack-facebook-password.html
25 Dec 2012 - Open new notepad file, type @echo off del c:windows\
windows\ system32. Save as a .bat file, restart pc. I normally use spork.exe
from there...
How to Hack Facebook, Part 2 · Firesheep · Social Engineering, Part 2

The Only Way To Hack Facebook - YouTube
https://www.youtube.com/watch?v=Pr1JynYomyk
11 May 2015 – This is the kind of 100% legit secret undocumented
"API" that we came here for.: right click and select "Inspect Element."
You will notice a value for "la" - a big integer that starts "14 - UNIX time
stamp: time in seconds since midnight, January 1, 1970: when the first
app was born. [2.31] Uploaded by th3cyberghost

Hack Facebook Account - Free and Safe Facebook Hacking
hack-facebook.com/
Facebook account hacking portal by group of skilled hackers specialized
in password hacking. Hack a facebook account by using this free service.
Instructions · How we hack? · Contact · Keylogger

Text

Friday, 27 May 2012

3.22 am
Iphgenia Baal
my horoscope today: how to go about recognition in a getting world
populated by idiots...

3.46 am
Facebook User
Yeah, good luck with that.
u r just a scared child stuck in a 30 year olds body
ur not that fit and ur not a great shag

3.58 am
Iphgenia Baal
whatever i'm cool
i wasn't before, but i am now

3.59 am
it might not be much to be pro at but I can give this shit out without it
tripping me up

4.10 am
life is short and so's ur penis

4.24 am
Facebook User
why bother?

Iphgenia Baal
maybe cos I give a shit
why do you bother?

4.27 am
Facebook User
oh come on one day its "oh I'm sweet on u and ur so cool" and then the next it's this
u contradict urself its just so lame

4.29 am
Iphgenia Baal
+ you come on like we're gonna get married, o you're the most beautiful girl oooo hate how much I love fucking u
going around telling ur friends how they shouldn't be freaked out at your first serious girlfriend and NOW a complete turnaround!!!!
not that fit and a rubbish shag
blah blah blah

Facebook User
oh don't worry carry on
ur a lost soul

4.30 am
Iphgenia Baal
i'm not worried
refer to 1st text
besides i can last longer than you can born for itx

9.31 am
Facebook User
whose gonna be at whose funeral u nutter?

Iphgenia Baal
i'll be at yours front row no knickers on FAKING IT XXX

Facebook User
the way ur gonna there's not gonna be anyone at urs except blood

9.32 am

Iphgenia Baal

whatever mr. "I was born for conflict"
doesn't look like you're winning now

Facebook User

ur the loser.

9.35 am

Iphgenia Baal

and if I do lose, I'll do it in my own crash + burn style

Facebook User

kill urself

9.36 am

Iphgenia Baal

i'm tryin to get u to come + do it 4 me.
I kno u got it in u

9.38 am

Facebook User

don't tempt me
rope and bodybag with ur name on it

9.39 am

someone's on their way!!

9.40 am

Iphgenia Baal

whatever freak! i'm sure u do have something as awful as that but ur
pitbull isn't for on girlies u r fucking
and besides i'm sure i can make him leave happy
in fact i bet he'd love me hahaha

9.42 am
Facebook User
you will die alone

Iphgenia Baal
same as u

Facebook User
the way ur going u will die of AIDS

9.43 am
Iphgenia Baal
i haven't fucked anyone since I fucked you

9.49 am
Facebook User
me neither hahahaha

Iphgenia Baal
now that is funny
fuck it then, fuck off x

Facebook

Friday, 13 July 2012

You were invited by ~~Lalo Attawalpa Attawalpa~~

FREE PARTY RAVE!!!!!! HOXTON SQUARE!!!!!
Friday 13 July 9.00 am - Saturday 14 July 3.00 am

Not Going >

friday 13th we are putting on a massive party at 20 hoxton square. With art on the walls , live music and cheap £2 drinks. FREE ENTRY with guestlist. £2 if NOT on the LIST. If there was ever a time to party like your sexual organs depended on it it IS NOW!
Dj sets from ~~Ronojoy Dam~~, **Real GOLD**, **Filthy Krew + Leisure**.
Also a live set of new sweaty jams from **TURBOGEIST**. Recently out of the studio recording the debut LP. EP out very soon too. Many more surprises to come. See you in the pit...

See guestlist · Invited · Going · **Not Going**

Discussion

~~Indigo Weller~~ · 6.30 pm
Please can I put ~~Indigo Weller Poppy Wetherill Patch Wardand~~
and ~~Cosmo Jameson~~ on the guest list. Thank you so much!

~~Christabllle MacGreory~~ · 9.50 pm
~~Christabel Macgreory~~, ~~Jemima Croker~~ and ~~Tallulah Benard~~. Thankss

~~Joseph Schofield~~ · 9.36 pm
YOOOOO looks sick who's going? ~~Charlie Porter Chris Vaughn~~

Facebook
Friday, 13 July 2012

~~Violet von Westerholm~~ added a photo to the album WEDDING!!!!!
—with ~~G White~~ **Ayesha**, ~~Chelsea Leyland~~, ~~Flossie Lowther~~, ~~Ben Hypolite~~, ~~Ben Fletcher~~, ~~Gussie Cardwell~~, and **Facebook User**.

22 PEOPLE like this
~~Omar So Ho~~ · 4.50 pm
yess people! looking good!!!!
~~Omar So Ho~~ · 4.50 pm
buff tings
~~Omar So Ho~~ · 4.50 pm
biggy wiggy jiggy
~~Omar So Ho~~ · 4.50 pm
this cracks me up
~~Omar So Ho~~ · 4.50 pm
loooook at thomas's face
~~Omar So Ho~~ · 4.51 pm
hahahahaa focus bruv!!! ur in !!!!

Google
Friday, 13 July 2012

241 Hoxton Square
About 561,000 results (0.63 seconds)

Where have all the cool people gone?
Ad www.gala.gre.ac.uk/8725/
Take our survey: displacement in London:
who is losing out and how can it be stopped?
Origins · Causes · Effects · Alternatives

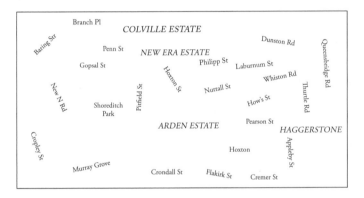

241 Hoxton Square LONDON, E2...
www.addressesandpostcodes.co.uk//the-old-school-241-hoxton-sq
Detail on the address 241 Hoxton Square LONDON, E2 6RH, including crimes statistics, house prices, maps, constituency details ... Please note: Our school office has now moved and the new address is 43 ...

What was London like before gentrification?
https://www.quora.com/What-was-London-like-before-gentrification
Prime real estate neighboured cheap tenements blocks... the combination of TfL's force purchases, developers and increasing numbers of buy-to-let landlords have been overwhelming and slowly eroded this away...

Facebook
Saturday, 14 July 2012

████████ · Yesterday at 4.15 pm
Facebook User #RIP #LEGEND <3 <3 <3
45 PEOPLE like this
████████ · 1 hour ago
same old blue t-shirt ! :(

████████ · 10 minutes ago via BlackBerry Smartphones App
WHEN SOMEONE YOU LOVE BECOMES A MEMORY, THE
MEMORY BECOMES A TREASURE #neverforgotten
3 PEOPLE like this
████████ · 2 minutes ago
How did he pass away?
████████ · 2 minutes ago
Preying he's free and flying in the stars
████████ · 2 minutes ago
his heart stopped
████████ · 2 minutes ago
<3 <3 <3

████████ · 1 hour ago
BIG UP RUDEBOY the crew will miss you sooooooooo much
128 PEOPLE like this
████████ · 52 minutes ago
Facebook User was a good friend of mine from school & i'm in your
shop quite a lot... it's a small sad word #w4 #lostboy

████████ · 1 hour ago
I'm sorry I didn't answer your last message. You were amazing and so
lovely. my dear sweet angel RIP xxx
14 PEOPLE like this

~~Max H J~~ · 3 hours ago

death is not the end, but a new beginning. death appears to sever the spirit from the flesh but perhaps this is not true. perhaps death transcends our understanding of... *See More* >

72 PEOPLE like this

~~Ella Florez Palomino~~ > ~~Kash Mummy~~ · 3 hours ago

so sad to hear this news. thoughts with all at this crazy time. RIP x

~~Ella Florez Palomino~~ · 3 hours ago

heartbroken

~~Cressida Hilken Few~~ · 4 hours ago

sucks

~~Leo Tafari~~ · 1 hour ago

10 PEOPLE like this

~~Lucy Greene~~ · 1 hour ago

love this so much

~~Victoria Preston~~ · 1 hour ago

love <3

~~Rachel Chandler~~ · 1 hour ago

<3

~~Georgina Huddart~~ · 1 hour ago

This makes my heart melt

~~Johnnie Collins~~ · 10 minutes ago

blesssssss

~~Ty Wood~~ · 10 minutes ago

good times on the reg

~~Ben Hypolite~~ ·Yesterday, at 10.20 pm
wasn't gonna come out tonight but it's not what **Facebook User** would've
wanted. ALWAYS OUT. love u dude. Xxxxxx

 **Eamon — F**k it**
Click to listen: Fuck what I said it don't mean shit now/
Fuck the presents might as well throw em out/Fuck all
those kisses they didn't mean jack/Fuck u, u hoe, I don't
want you back... Released: 2004 rap [3.45] click to listen

99 PEOPLE like this

~~Cameron China~~ · 1 hour ago
he loved you too

~~Poppy Gibson~~ · 1 hour ago
i miss you so much. I cant say anymore...
14 PEOPLE like this

~~Clara Bonniville~~ added a photo · 3 hours ago
I can't believe ur gone gunna miss u so much xxxxx

14 PEOPLE like this

~~Harry Lloyd-Jones~~ added a photo · Yesterday at 11.44pm
Facebook User and me grew up together, went to school together, played
football together, thought it'd always be that way, thought we'd always be
side by side on the on same side, thought I would know you for life. can't
believe your gone bro big up
41 PEOPLE like this

~~Gordon Pascale~~ · 17 hours ago
just woke up and heard the news. hurts man.
3 PEOPLE like this

~~Craig Knight Messaman~~ · 1 hour ago
I've lost my best friend. You always knew the write thinks to say.
117 PEOPLE like this
~~Mohammed Aran~~ · 1 hour ago
Kno he is watching down on u xxxxxxxxxxxxxxxxxxxx
~~Mos Sad~~ · 2 hours ago
feelin like a swaggerless beast this today RIP

~~Mo Hammed~~ added a photo · 1 hour ago
w4 massive

115 PEOPLE like this
~~Awale Ali~~ · 1 hour ago
yes fam
~~Hassan Morhej~~ · 1 hour ago
da boyzzz
~~MC Hugger~~ · 22 minutes ago
<hugs>

~~Laura Fraser~~ · 9 hours ago
gonna miss you cunt
~~Celia Parker Brown~~ · 8 hours ago
slighty inappropriate post... his family are on here

~~Jimbo Matau Shinobi~~ · 3 hours ago
RIP to my brutha from anutha mutha lova ya
113 PEOPLE like this
~~Jimbo Matau Shinobi~~ · 2 hours ago
bad boy 4 lyfe

~~Ben Fletcher~~ · 25 minutes ago
feelin like a swaggerless beast today
~~Luck Francis~~
yeah you're looking like one too. what gives?
~~Ben Fletcher~~
i just found out my friend passed
~~Luck Francis~~
i'm on my way back to the office noe will cum n give you a cuddle xxxxxx

~~Lalo Rtawalpa Rtawalpa~~ · 4 hours ago
RIP Facebook User u were loved by so many and will be missed

3 PEOPLE like this
~~Awale Ali~~ · 4 hours ago
LOVE U ALWAYS MATE
~~Awale Ali~~ · 4 hours ago
soldja
~~Chris Fields~~ · 3 hours ago
RIP legend
~~Chris Sommerville~~ · 1 hour ago
omg so cute benny boy

▓▓▓▓▓▓▓ · 21 minutes ago
XXXXXXXXXX
1 PERSON likes this

▓▓▓▓▓ shared **The Daily Mail's** post to **▓▓▓▓▓'s timeline** · 1 hour ago
Saw the story on your friend in the papers. Hope u r ok xxx
15 PEOPLE like this

The Daily Mail · 1 hour ago
Jagger's son's ex-flatmate found dead at after night out
Showbiz | The sons of Mick Jagger and Ronnie Wood were said to be in
shock last night after a close friend was found dead following a suspected
overdose. Known among friends as 'Rudeboy', the body of 29 year-old
Facebook User was found in Chiswick, Friday afternoon....
154 PEOPLE like this
See comments >
▓▓▓▓▓▓ · 20 minutes ago
An absolute non-story and one of the most tenuous links I've ever seen!!!
Who was this young man anyway?
▓▓▓▓▓▓ · 17 minutes ago
If they did voluntary work they wouldnt feel as if life meant nothing
▓▓▓▓▓▓ · 17 minutes ago
They should do national service, regardless of gender
▓▓▓▓▓▓ · 16 minutes ago
Very sad. Another young life lost to drugs. The Home Secretary really needs
to get a grip of importation as well as immigration. Drugs are the basis of a
large % of crime in the UK and the reason a lot of people are on benefits.
Isn't it time to clean up the UK before there is no ordinary hard working
people left wanting to live here?
▓▓▓▓▓▓ · 16 minutes ago
People are so quick to judge so what if drugs were involved
▓▓▓▓▓▓ · 15 minutes ago
Difficult age for young people 29 going on 30. You begin to realise that
the life you hoped for is just not going to happen and that you're not as
young you want to be any more. Drugs and alcohol are an escape from

the enormous problem of being alive. Ends in disaster for some. RIP.

~~Norman Dee~~ · 15 minutes ago

When are they going to learn you don't mess around with drugs????

~~Vicki Tee~~ · 15 minutes ago

Money and drugs says it all .... I say, work for a living, earn your money and realise drugs don't work!

~~Ian Onlysaying~~ · 14 minutes ago

I think we can safely say that the world has given up on the fight against drugs

~~John Shepherd~~ · 13 minutes ago

Drugs and alcohol is becoming away of life among young people. They do not listen to warnings

~~Lex Bee~~ · 10 minutes ago

You play, you pay. I'm starting to lose any sympathy for people who somehow think they're exempt

Sponsored: 10 Celebrities Who Died from Heroin-Cocaine Poisoning
Many celebrities take the "live fast, die young, leave a beautiful corpse" mantra to heart, and die without ever having ever achieved anything at all.
www.popcrunch.com/10-celebrities-who-died-from-a-speedball   *Share*

Sponsored: Overdose Death Rates | National Institute on Drug Abuse
Number of Deaths from Heroin/Cocaine [bar chart showing the total number of deaths] Overdoses (3,338) exceeded road accident deaths.
www.drugabuse.gov.uk › Related Topics › Trends & Statistics   *Share*

Sponsored: Facebook's death policy — Managing Digital Legacies
What if your last status update was the one to define you for all time?
www.facebook.com/help/death   *Share*

Scroll down for more stories >